掌握英文寫作格式

笹井常三 著

林秀如 譯

A Stylebook for English Writing

三民書局

前　言

　　對於我國的英語教育，批判的言論一直未曾停歇，其中又以「大學畢業了卻連一句像樣的英文都說不出口」的抨擊最為強烈，反而比較少聽到「無法寫出像樣的英文」之類的言論。這是否意味著國人英文的「書寫」能力比英文「會話」能力「好一點」呢？筆者並不以為然。

　　大學的入學考試一直被視為英語教育「缺陷」的元兇，其評分非常耗時，而且受限於電腦閱卷大量處理答案的符號選擇方式，因而產生目前這種出題方向儘量避免需要寫英文的情況。雖然有人呼籲：在國際化的時代裡，傳達個人思想的「發信型英語是必要的」，但事實上願意提筆「寫英文」的人卻是少之又少。

　　即使在大學「英文寫作」的課程中，大部分仍然採取從教科書中節選出數句沒有關聯的句子並將其翻成英文的測驗模式，很少有學校願意在初期花兩三個小時來教授英文寫作的第一步——punctuation（標點符號用法）。常聽到有人說寫英文只要大意通順就好了，但事實上並非如此。首先，要了解英文寫作的最基本法則，而且必須遵守。否則，不但無法完整地表達

出自己的意思，反而有時容易招致誤解，或甚至因此產生失禮於對方等不合宜的情形。這麼一來，刻意的溝通也就變得毫無意義了。

本書在 Part 1 中多方收錄英文書寫的 「法則」，尤其是 punctuation 方面會舉實例說明。這些雖說是法則，實際上當然沒有法律上的強制力。不過，若忽視了寫作法則，就會有上述不合宜的情況發生。衷心希望各位能了解法則，並進而遵守。

Part 2 將提出「大寫」、「拼字」及「數字」的用法等，試圖再鞏固各位英文寫作的基礎。

Part 3 是筆者根據長年在報社擔任英文記者，以及之後教學所累積的經驗下，針對英文寫作所提出的若干詳盡的備忘錄。礙於篇幅，僅擷取重要的主題做說明，若能提供對英文寫作有興趣的讀者一點參考，便感相當欣慰。

至於專欄 Coffee Break，就如同字面所示，希望各位能以一邊喝咖啡或喝茶的悠閒心情來閱讀。

最後，在此謹向為本書出版不遺餘力的研究社出版部佐藤淳先生，致上吾人最深的謝意。

1999 年 5 月

笹井 常三

前言

Part 1
標點符號

① 段首

　　段首，正確來說就是段落 (paragraph) 的開始，一般英文寫作的正確標準格式是留五個空格 (space)，稱為首行縮排 (indentation *or* indention)，步驟是使鍵盤 (keyboard) 呈半形輸入模式，再按五次空白鍵 (space key)。(編者按：臺灣通常是空四格)

　　現今個人電腦 (personal computer) 都備有可以讓游標 (cursor) 一次移動一個事先設定好欄位的 Tab (= tabulator) 鍵。只要設定好縮排的位移格數再按下確認鍵 (return key *or* enter key)，馬上就能產生縮排。

　　縮排會在每次更換段落，也就是換行時產生。近來，在各種報告、文章，以及商業書信中，已經有愈來愈多人不使用縮排。在這種情形之下，就要空一行 (double space)，然後再繼續下一個段落。

　　大多數的個人電腦，都附有將一行內的文字和數字間的字距平等均分，並統一行末的功能。只要利用齊行功能 (justification)，就不須因為行尾空間不夠，而硬把一個單字拆開分成兩行 (如後所述，會伴隨不知從哪裡斷字的麻煩問題，請參照「連字號」說明)。

　　特別是撰寫論文，若要放入很長的引用文並需要換行或縮排時，在每一行的行尾也要反方向做五格縮排。引用文結束後回到本文時同樣要換行。也就是會變成引用文全文的左右兩邊都依本文的縮排位移格數往內縮的情形。另外，除非引用文本身有引號 (quotation marks)，否則在引用文部分不須另加引號。

　　書籍、報章雜誌因為各有其編輯的風格，所以關於縮排並

無既定的規則。有的出版物是空三格 (stroke)，有的是空五格，也有的是將每一章節第一個段落的前三個字或前五個字全部設定為大寫 (all caps)。

　　撰寫原稿時，若無特殊需求，只要依照本章開頭所敘述的方式做縮排，其他的交由編輯編排即可。

2　句點 (period)　　　　．

　　period 主要為美語說法；英語則是用 full stop, full point 表示，或者簡稱 dot。

　　句點的主要功能如下：

1. 置於句子的最後
2. 接在縮寫字之後
3. 做為小數點 (decimal point) 使用
4. 用於省略符號 (ellipsis)（請參照「省略符號」說明）

（1）　置於句子 (sentence) 的最後。但不包括疑問句 (interrogative sentence) 及感嘆句 (exclamatory sentence) 的句子。

She is a high school student.

I want to brush up on my English.（我想要溫習英文。）

Keep the door closed.

Don't forget to lock the door when you go out.

注：Internet（網際網路）上的 home page（首頁）或 e-mail（電
子郵件）地址中的 . 讀做 dot [dɑt]。例如，BBC 的網址
www.bbc.co.uk/ 就讀做 www dot bbc dot co[ko] dot uk

slash。

（2） 接在縮寫字之後。但通常不會接在頭字語 (acronym) 之後。（請參照 Part 2「縮寫字與頭字語」說明）

Mon. = Monday　　　Nov. = November

Washington, D.C. (D.C. = District of Columbia)（美國首都華盛頓特區）

U.K. (UK = United Kingdom)（英國）

Gen. (= General) Douglas MacArthur（將軍）

Adm. (= Admiral) Isoroku Yamamoto（艦隊司令官）

St. (= Saint) John（聖徒，聖人）

Rev. (= Reverend) Arthur Dimmesdale（教士，牧師）

注 1：ASEAN（= Association of Southeast Asian Nations 東南亞國協）、OPEC（= Organization of Petroleum Exporting Countries 石油輸出國家組織）便是頭字語。ASEAN 的唸法不是 A [e] S [ɛs] E [i] A [e] N [ɛn] 一個字母一個字母地唸，而是視為一個單字唸成 [ˋæsɪən]。同樣地，OPEC 則唸成 [oˋpɛk]。

注 2：對於縮寫字的後面是否要接句點，英國和美國有很大的差異。以前的英式寫法通常是 Mister (Mr) 或 Doctor (Dr) 後面還留有文字時，不加句點；但如今也漸漸地在其他的縮寫字後頭不加句點。舉些例子來看：

	英式	美式
Mister	Mr	Mr.
Mistress	Ms	Mrs.
Doctor	Dr	Dr.

Sunday	Sun	Sun.
Monday	Mon	Mon.
January	Jan	Jan.
February	Feb	Feb.
manuscript	Ms	Ms.
company	Co	Co.
corporation	Corp	Corp.

注 3 ：句子若在縮寫字結束時，不加句點。

The college offers a program leading to M.A. [不寫成 M.A..]

The "nuclear club" includes Russia and the U.S. [不寫成 U.S..]

（3） 接在人名的起首字母 (initials) 之後。

Harry S. Truman　　John F. Kennedy

E. H. Carr　　　　　O. J. Simpson

（4） 做為小數點使用（這時通常讀做 point。但是 .5 也可唸成 and a half）。

0.3　　　(zero point three/[英] nought point three)

3.8　　　(three point eight)

6.5　　　(six point five)

15.34　　(fifteen point three four/fifteen point thirty-four)

The temperature soared to 38.8 degrees C., a high for the season.

（氣溫上升到今夏的最高溫 38.8 度。）

（5） 做為貨幣金額的基本單位和其以下單位的劃分點。閱讀時通常會將基本單位以下的名稱省略。此外，日圓(yen)、中國貨幣(yuan)、韓國貨幣(won)都是單複數同形。

The dollar was worth ¥135.65. (one hundred thirty-five point sixty-five yen *or* one hundred thirty-five yen and sixty-five sen)

The CD-ROM cost $85.95. (eighty-five point ninety-five dollars *or* eighty-five dollars [and] ninety-five cents)

3 逗點 (comma) ,

逗點的主要功能是在劃分句子中對等 (coordinate) 的單字 (word)、片語 (phrase) 及子句 (clause)，或區分從屬的片語和子句。除此之外，當然也有其他功能。

（1） 連續使用三個以上同一詞類的單字時，在每個單字後加上逗點。最後兩個單字之間通常用 and 或 or 連接，且 and 或 or 前面須加逗點，以避免句意上的混淆。不過，若句子本身的意義明確，可以不加逗點。

The Italian national flag is green, white(,) and red.

You can choose any of the three colors—green, white(,) or red.

He is a tall and handsome businessman with a good command of English, French(,) and German. （他是個又高又帥的企業家，而且精通英語、法語和德語。）

'I have nothing to offer but blood, toil, tears and sweat.' —[Churchill-1] （我所能付出的只有血、勞力、淚和汗水。）

注 1：並列一連串的片語或者三個以上的子句時，在每個片語或子句後面加上逗點。

注 2：He is a tall and handsome businessman. 也可寫成 He is a tall, handsome businessman.。但是在 young, old, little 之前通常不用逗點。

She is a refined young woman. （她是位有教養的年輕女性。）

（2） 置於副詞片語 (adverbial phrase) 及副詞子句 (adverbial clause) 之後。若主要子句 (principal clause) 在前面，則放在主要子句的後面。

Strangely enough, she turned up far ahead of all others. （奇怪的是，她出現得比其他所有的人還來得早。）

However hard you may try, you won't get it done in a day. （不管你多麼努力，一天之內是不可能做完的。）

You won't get it done in a day, no matter how hard you may try. [主要子句在前]

If conditions permit, we will get the project under way in less than a month. （若情況允許，我們將可在一個月之內著手進行此項計劃。）

（3） 接在獨立不定詞 (absolute infinitive) 或獨立分詞 (absolute participle) 之後。

To be honest, he doesn't deserve your respect. （說老實話，他並不值得你尊重。）

Generally speaking, young men are better off than their

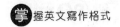

parents. （一般而言，年輕人比他們的父母親生活寬裕。）

（4）　放在稱呼語之前或之後。

"Why are you so late, John?"

Ladies and gentlemen, it's my great honor to welcome you to our new head office. （各位女士、先生，非常榮幸能歡迎各位蒞臨我們的新總公司。）

（5）　用於表示同位語 (appositive)，前後各放一個逗點。

John F. Kennedy, 35th president of the United States, was 46 when he was assassinated. （美國第 35 任總統約翰·甘迺迪在 46 歲時遭到暗殺。）

Japan, a co-sponsor of the resolution, called for quick ratification of the treaty. （決議案的共同提案國日本要求提早通過該項條約。）

（6）　放在插入語 (parenthesis) 的前後。

She lived, as it were, in a fish bowl. （說起來她就像住在魚缸裡的人。）

"Jean, to tell the truth, you're not equal to the job." （珍，說真的，妳無法勝任這份工作。）

Developing nations, let me assure you, have become more aware of the need for international cooperation in reducing emission gases. （我在此鄭重宣佈，開發中國家已經意識到要減少排放廢氣就必須結合國際間的協助。）

（7） 置於直接引述 (direct narration) 中的傳述子句 (reporting clause) 和傳述詞 (reported speech) 之間。

He said, "I can't stand this any more." （他說：「我再也無法忍受了。」）

"This is outrageous," he shouted, "this should stop!" （他叫喊著：「這太過分了，應該要停止！」）

> 注：有時也會用冒號代替逗點，如 He said: "I can't stand this any more."，但被傳述的詞句通常會換行。

（8） 置於 yes 和 no 之後。

She replied, "Yes, I'll be delighted to come."

"No, I didn't do it," he protested.

"No, no, I didn't mean that."

（9） 置於感嘆詞 (interjection) 之後。

"Well, this is what happened."

"Oh, let's get together sometime."

"Why, isn't that funny — my name's Miriam, too." — [Capote] （哇，真有意思。我也叫米瑞安呢！）

> 注：除了上述感嘆詞之外，還有 ah, aha, come on, look, my, oh my, uh, uh huh 等。

（10） 置於附加問句 (tag question) 之前。

You know him, don't you?

He didn't do it, did he?

（11）　關係代名詞 (relative pronoun) 接在先行詞 (antecedent) 之後做附加說明時，會使用逗點。雖然這是非限定的用法 (non-restrictive use)，但一般而言，都會在關係代名詞之前加上逗點。

She has four grandchildren, who are all in their 20s.（她有四個孫子，都是 20 多歲。）

He said he would do his best, which was simply not true.（他說他會盡力而為，其實根本是在說謊。）

（12）　置於形容詞、分詞之前或之後。

He stood there, speechless.（他不發一語地站在那裡。）

Undeterred by threats, he made the report public.（他不畏威脅地將報告公開。）

Once lost, moral authority is almost impossible to recapture.（一旦失去道德的權威，就很難再挽回。）

（13）　放在人名後面的年齡數字之前及之後。

James Turner, 38, and his son Jerry, 7, were among those rescued from the burning ferry.

（14）　用來隔開鄉鎮名、縣市（州）名和國家名。這時，順序要由小寫到大。

He was born in Takatsuki City, Osaka Prefecture.

She attended a San Jose, California(,) high school.

（15）　用於明確區分所屬機構及地址等。

Manfred Weiss, Assistant Manager, Export Division, Evian Trading Corporation

His address: 123, Minami 3-chome, Kishibe, Suita City, Osaka, 564–8511, Japan

（16） 用於區分年、月、日等。

He was born on July 4, 1975.

The contest will be held on Wednesday, January 15, beginning at 10 a.m.

（17） 用於區別運動比賽的得分。

Yakult Swallows 6, Hanshin Tigers 4

Maple Leafs 7, Penguins 1

Southampton 3, Wimbledon 1

4 冒號 (colon) ：

冒號的主要功能是在句子的結尾加入明細和說明。

（1） 除了接在冒號之後的第一個單字是專有名詞或是一個完整句子的第一個字母要大寫外，其他情形皆為小寫。

We have to wage a struggle against the common enemies of mankind: tyranny, poverty, disease and war itself.—[JFK]（我們必須對抗人類的共通敵人，也就是要對抗專制、貧窮、疾病以及戰爭本身。）

（2）　放在 as follows 和 the following 所引導的句子前，或者放在作用和其相當的詞語所引導的句子前。若引用的內容過長時，則應該換行。

He said as follows: "Japan should continue to press for the abolition of nuclear weapons."（他如此說道：「日本應該繼續強烈要求廢除核武。」）

He made the following remarks: "Japan should continue...."

He had this to say on the subject: "Japan should continue...."

注：引用句若跨越兩個以上的段落時，各段落之前要加 opening quotation marks（"），不過 closing quotation marks（"）只用在最後一個段落。

（3）　say 或意思類似的動詞之後接直接引述時，一般會以逗點區分開來，但有時也會使用冒號，而且通常會換行。

For example, in 1933, President Franklin Roosevelt told the country: "The only thing we have to fear is fear itself." —[*VOA*]（例如，1933年美國總統富蘭克林‧羅斯福曾說過：「唯一我們應該感到恐懼的，就是恐懼本身。」）

She said very quietly and slowly:

"He's worth everything in the world to me." —[Christie]（她冷靜且緩緩地說：「他對我來說，是世界上最重要的人。」）

（4）　在摘要前文或後文的內容時使用。

The main burden of his speech is: Japan should demand a total ban on nuclear tests.（他的演講主旨是：日本應該要求全面禁

止核武試驗。）

One thing I am sure of is this: The less said, the better. （我確信一件事：少說多益。）

（5） 用於強調。

We abate nothing of our just demands: not one jot or tittle do we recede.—[Churchill-2] （我們堅持我們的正當要求，一步也不退讓。）

（6） 指出《聖經》的章 (chapter)、節 (verse)。

But Jesus said to him, 'Put up your sword. All who take the sword die by the sword.' (Matthew 26:52) （但耶穌對他說：「將你的劍收入劍鞘吧。所有持劍之人皆會亡於劍下。」）〔〈馬太福音〉第 26 章第 52 節〕

（7） 在戲劇、訴訟或記者會活動的互相對答內容上，標示於詢問者及回答者之後。為求方便閱讀，人名以黑體字 (boldface) 顯示，另外冒號與對答內容之間通常會留空格。

下面是 1998 年 9 月 11 日公布的對話內容，是從獨立檢察官 (Independent Counsel) Kenneth Starr 對美國總統柯林頓所做的報告書中摘錄下來。Q 代表控告總統性騷擾的 Paula Jones 的律師，WJC 代表美國總統 William Jefferson Clinton 的縮寫。

Q: Well, have you given any gifts to Monica Lewinsky? （那麼，你曾經送過禮物給莫妮卡·陸文斯基嗎？）

WJC: I don't recall. Do you know what they were? （我沒有印

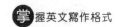

象了。你知道是什麼東西嗎？）

Q: A hat pin?（一個女帽的別針吧？）

WJC: I don't, I don't remember. But I certainly, I could have.（不，我不記得了。不過，也許真的送過吧。）

Q: A book about Walter Whitman?（那華特‧惠特曼寫的書呢？）

WJC: I give—let me just say, I give people a lot of gifts, and when people are around I give a lot of things at the White House away, so I could have given her a gift, but I don't remember a specific gift.（我這麼說吧：我給過別人很多東西，在白宮也送過不少禮物給身邊的人。所以有可能送過她禮物，但是不記得是什麼特別的東西了。）

（8） 表示競賽記錄的時間。

Japan's Naoko Takahashi won the women's marathon in 2 hours, 21 minutes, 47 seconds. The 26-year-old runner renewed her own Japanese record of 2:25:48 set in Nagoya in March. Her compatriot Tomoko Kai finished third in 2:35:1.（日本選手高橋尚子以 2 小時 21 分 47 秒贏得女子馬拉松比賽的冠軍。26 歲的高橋刷新了 3 月在名古屋所創的 2 小時 25 分 48 秒的日本記錄。而同樣來自日本的早斐智子則以 2 小時 35 分 1 秒奪得第三名。）

（9） 表示一天的時間。

The plane took off at 11:45 a.m. and was due to land at Kansai International Airport at 3:15 p.m.（本機於上午 11 時 45 分起

飛，預計將於下午 3 時 15 分抵達關西國際機場。）

注：也可用句點代替冒號，如 11.45。

（10） 放在書信開頭的稱呼語 (salutation) 之後。

Dear Sirs:

Gentlemen:

Attention: Mr. Yoshida, Sales Manager

To Whom It May Concern:（敬啟者）

注：在英國則以逗點取代冒號使用。

（11） 用於 e-mail 及備忘錄。

Subject: Midterm test

To: Ms. Hanako Kimura

From: Ichiro Suzuki

5 分號 (semicolon) ;

分號所表達的分開意思會比逗點更明顯。

（1） 連結兩個獨立子句，並強調其關聯性。

Happiness lies not in the mere possession of money; it lies in the joy of achievement, in the thrill of creative effort.（幸福不完全是來自財富，而是來自成就的喜悅和創造成果的雀躍心情。）

Each increase of tension has produced an increase of arms; each increase of arms has produced an increase of tension. —[JFK]

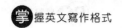

（每當情勢一緊張就會加強軍備；每當軍備加強時就加深情勢的緊張。）

注：上述例句可用句點取代分號，變成兩個獨立的句子，也可以用「逗點＋and」替代，形成一個複合句 (compound sentence)。但若要更明確顯示兩個子句內容的相關性時，則用分號。

（２）　用於句子中有很多詞語和數字並列時，為避免使用過多的逗點產生混淆，而另外使用分號區隔。

He has three children—Jack, 18, a college student; Grace, 16, a high school student; and Rose, 11, a sixth-grader. （他有三個小孩──傑克，18 歲，大學生；葛蕾絲，16 歲，高中生；蘿絲，11 歲，小學六年級學生。）

Its [The Watergate's] tenants included the former Attorney General of the United States John N. Mitchell, now director of the Committee for the Re-election of the President; the former Secretary of Commerce Maurice H. Stans, finance chairman of the President's campaign; the Republican national chairman, Senator Robert Dole of Kansas; President Nixon's secretary, Rose Mary Woods; and Anna Chennault, who was the widow of Flying Tiger ace Claire Chennault and a celebrated Republican hostess; plus many other prominent figures of the Nixon administration.—[Bernstein] （住在「水門綜合大廈」裡的人包括──前美國聯邦政府首席檢察官，現任總統改選委員會主任委員 John N. Mitchell；前貿易部長，現任總統大選財政首長 Maurice H. Stans；共和黨全國委員會主委兼堪薩斯州參議

員 Robert Dole；尼克森總統秘書 Rose Mary Woods；[二次世
界大戰中，為協助中國對日抗戰而組成的]美軍飛虎隊傑出飛
行員陳納德的遺孀，同時也是著名的共和黨女性領導人陳香
梅，以及多位尼克森政權的高級官員。）

（3）　以 besides, consequently, hence, however, moreover, other-
wise, still, therefore, thus, yet 等副詞連接兩個子句時，將分號
置於副詞之前。也可以將分號置於 for example, for instance,
that is 等片語之前。

She is beautiful; besides, she is fabulously rich.

The condo had a high price tag; moreover, it was quite far from
the nearest railroad station.（這間有獨立產權的公寓價格很高，
而且離最近的車站相當遠。）

注：上述副詞亦稱為連接副詞 (conjunctive adverb)。

6 問號 (question mark)　?

亦可稱為 interrogation point 或 interrogation mark。

（1）　接在疑問句 (interrogative sentence) 之後。

How are you, John?

Where are you from?

Did you enjoy yourself?

注：疑問句若為句子的一部分，即為陳述句 (declarative
sentence)，結束時用句點。

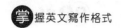

He asked me where I was from.

He asked me if I had enjoyed myself.

（2）　當疑問詞 (interrogative) 只有一個單字，或和其他詞語連結也不構成一個完整的句子時，必須使用問號。

Who?	What?	When?
Why?	Where?	How?
For whom?	What for?	Since when?
Why not?	From where?	How much?

（3）　雖然是陳述句，但內容相當於疑問句時，要加問號。這種情形經常可在口語會話式的句子中見到。

You have to go so soon?

"She—she—is asking for me? I'll—I'll come—at once."—[Christie] （她…她想見我？我…我馬上過去。）

（4）　但內容和請求 (request) 有關的句子，即使形式上為疑問句，也可以不用問號。

Would you please pick me up at the hotel.

（5）　使用於對該句中的字或年代有疑問時，含有不確定之意在內。

b. AD 170?—d. 229? （生於西元 170 年？死於西元 229 年？）

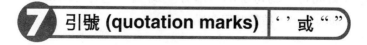

7 引號 (quotation marks) 　' ' 或 " "

亦可稱為 quotes 或 inverted commas。英式語法中，單引號 ' '(single quotation marks) 和雙引號 " "(double quotation marks) 兩種均可使用，但美式語法主要使用雙引號。

　　前面的引號（"）稱之為 open-quote marks，後面的引號（"）則稱為 close-quote marks。

　　引號主要用於直接引用他人的陳述或所寫的字句。當然，另有其他功能如後述。

　　使用引號的原則如下：

・句點和逗點放在引號內。

He described the situation as "very serious."

"I'm so happy to see you," he said.

注：英式語法則較常將句點和逗點放在引號外。

・冒號和分號放在引號外。

He said, "I'm too tired to walk"; however, he was on his feet again in a second.

・? 和 ! 放在引號內。但是，若引用的部分並非完整的疑問句或感嘆句時，則放在引號外。

"Do I have to go?" she asked.

Did she really say, "I have to go"?

　　使用 double quotation marks 後，若其中要再插入引用句時要用 single quotation marks。相反地，以 single quotations 開始的句子，中間要再插入引用句時，則用 double quotation marks。

（1）置於直接引述之前後。直接引述的第一個字母為大寫

(capital letter *or* upper case)。若直接引述中間插入如 said the man, I said 等詞語時，則接在後面的第一個字母為小寫 (small letter *or* lower case)。

She said, "I'm hungry."

He shouted, "Leave me alone!"

"Yes, she is very rich," said the man, "but she is lonely."

"Then you don't believe," I said, "that he shot himself?"— [Christie]（我說：「那麼你是不相信他是舉槍自盡的囉？」）

The newspaper quoted the prime minister as saying, "We'll do all in our power to put the economy back on the road to recovery."（該報導引用首相的談話：「我們將傾全力促使經濟復甦。」）

注：當我們引述他人的詞語或句子時，如廣播、電視節目或直接以聲音傳達給聽者的情況下，為了明確突顯引用句，通常會在引用之前說 "and I quote" 或 "I quote"，甚至也有只說 "quote"（開始引用）。最後在引用結束時會說 unquote（結束引用）。

就上一個例句來說，唸到 The newspaper quoted the prime minister as saying 時，就可以小聲唸出 "and I quote", "I quote" 或 "quote"，短暫停頓之後再讀出引用句。讀完引用句後，通常無須再停頓，直接唸出 "unquote" 即可。不過，由於聽眾通常都知道哪些是引用句，因此大多可以省略 "unquote"。

（2） 用於明確顯示各項訊息。

Shops throughout the European Union already are displaying

"We accept euros" signs.—[*Time*] （歐盟國家已經到處都有商店掛出「我們接受歐元」的告示牌。）

（3） 置於解釋定義或說明性的詞語之前後。

Dares Salaam, capital of Tanzania, means "haven of peace." （坦尚尼亞的首都三蘭港，意指「和平之港」。）

A "cold fish" is not a fish. It is a person. But it is a person who is unfriendly, unemotional and shows no love or warmth.—[*VOA*] （"cold fish" 不是指魚，而是指人類。但指的是那種不友善、不付出情感、令人感受不到流露出愛與溫暖的人。）

The expression "burning your bridges" means acting in such a way that you destroy any chance of turning back or changing your decision.—[*VOA*] （"burning your bridges" [破釜沈舟，背水一戰] 的意思是，破壞任何可以回頭或改變決定的可能性後，所採取的行動。）

（4） 用來表示書籍中收錄的短篇作品、報章雜誌的報導及論文的標題，或詩名、歌曲名，以及各個電視節目的名稱。書籍、雜誌以及主要音樂作品本身的名稱則用斜體字 (italics)。手寫時，改用劃底線的方式表示。

Capote, Truman. "Miriam," *A Tree of Night and Other Stories* [*A Tree of Night and Other Stories* 為書名，而 "Miriam" 是其中的短篇作品]

Vogel, Ezra F. "Pax Nipponica?" *Foreign Affairs*, Spring 1986 ["Pax Nipponica?" 為報導的標題。*Foreign Affairs* 是書刊名]

Buchwald, Art. "U.S. vs. the Land of the Rising Sony," *Los*

Angeles Times, Apr. 7, 1987 ["U.S. vs. the Land of the Rising Sony" 為刊登在報紙上的論文名]

A common assignment is to watch the news panel shows—"Face the Nation," "Issues and Answers" and "Meet the Press"—and take notes on what the guests say.—[*WP*]（一般的課外作業是觀看新聞座談性的節目，如 "Face the Nation", "Issues and Answers", "Meet the Press" 等，然後再將來賓的言論記錄下來。）

> 注：戲劇人物、報紙、雜誌及其他定期性刊物、船舶，以及動物的名稱則不加引號。

（5） 演講、傳教性的議題名稱及手冊的標題等也使用引號。

He won the English oratorical contest with a speech titled "Political Apathy Among College Students."（他以「大學生不關心政治」為題的演說贏得英語演講比賽的第一名。）

Dr. Martin Luther King delivered his famous "I Have a Dream" speech before a crowd of 200,000 people surrounding the steps of the Lincoln Memorial in Washington, D.C. on August 28, 1968.（馬丁·路德·金恩博士在 1968 年 8 月 28 日於華盛頓擠滿 20 萬群眾的林肯紀念堂，發表了有名的演說「我還有夢」。）

（6） 有意表示強調、幽默、諷刺時使用。

This is a "must have" book for every home.（這是每個家庭「必備」的書。）

He is the "conscience of Japan."（他代表的是「日本的良心」。）

（7）　表示綽號、藝名。

Nat "King" Cole was a popular American jazz singer and pianist in the early 1940's. (Nat "King" Cole 是 1940 年代初期美國非常受歡迎的爵士歌手及鋼琴家。)

Virgil "the Turk" Sollozzo was a powerfully built, medium-sized man of dark complexion who could have been taken for a true Turk.—[Puzo]（Virgil "the Turk" Sollozzo 是位體格強壯、中等身材、皮膚黝黑的男子，就像是位真正的土耳其人。）

（8）　為避免引用過長的句子，一般會以五行、一百個字或者兩個句子左右做為適當的長度。另外，例如從演講中引用的句子若跨越兩個以上的段落時，須在各個段落的開頭前加上引號，但該段落結束時則不加，而於最後段落的結尾處再加上引號即可。

注：關於論文的引用，請參照「段首」說明。

掌握鉛字的「大小」祕密

現今萬能的電腦已經可以提供各式各樣印刷的字級和字體。在早年（雖說如此，也還不到三十年前的事）以鉛字印製報紙的年代裡，與其說字為「文字」，還不如說是「鉛字」來得恰當。

　　雖說現今是電腦萬能的時代，只要幾個按鍵就能輕輕鬆鬆變化文字、編排好文章的版面，然而，若能多少了解一些關於文字和印刷方面的事，也是蠻有趣又有益的。

　　先要了解英文字母中字體大小的單位是點 (point)。72 點的文字長度為 1 英寸（約 2.54 公分）。36 點的文字則是二分之一英寸，24 點為三分之一英寸。報紙的報導所使用的文字大概是 8 點，廣播電臺、電視節目表則大多為小小的 6 點。

　　寫標題（head 或 headline）時，最麻煩的就是每個字母的寬度問題。即便是同樣的大寫字母，M 和 W 就屬於 fat letters（胖體字），比 A, B 寬；小寫字裡 m, w 也比 a, b 寬。而大寫的 I 和小寫的 f, i, j, l, r, t 都屬於 thin letters（瘦體字）。

　　對於字母的寬度有一定的了解後，除了可以幫助我們寫標題時避免所有的字母跑出欄位 (column) 外，亦可同時做好版面的配置。下面介紹字母的寬度標準。

以 1/2（單位）計算的字母及符號：
f, i, j, l, r, t（所謂的 thin letters）
標點符號（punctuation marks）。不過，破折號 (dash —) 為 1 又 1/2，雙引號 (double quotation marks " ") 以及問號 (?) 為 1。
空白鍵通常也算做 1/2。

以 1（單位）計算的字母及符號：
大寫字母 I, J

小寫字母（不包含 f, i, j, l, r, t 及 m, w）

所有的數字 (figures)

以 1 又 1/2（單位）計算的字母及符號：

大寫字母（不包含M, W 及 I, J）

小寫字母 m, w

破折號（一）

以 2（單位）計算的字母及符號：

大寫字母 M, W

例：請計算出下列標題的總寬度。

$$1\quad 1\quad \tfrac{1}{2}\ \underset{1\tfrac{1}{2}\ \ 1\ \ \tfrac{1}{2}\ \ 1\ \ \tfrac{1}{2}\ \ 1\ \ 1\quad \tfrac{1}{2}}{}\ \underset{}{}\ 1\tfrac{1}{2}\ \tfrac{1}{2}\ \ 1\ \ 1\ \ 1\quad \underset{\tfrac{1}{2}\ \ 1\tfrac{1}{2}\ \tfrac{1}{2}\ \ 1\ \ 1\ \ 1}{}= 20$$

30 Survive Plane Crash

8　撇號 (apostrophe)　　　，

撇號有以下三項功能：

　1. 構成名詞 (noun) 及特定的代名詞 (pronoun) 的所有格。

　2. 用於表示動詞片語 (verb phrase) 及數字 (figures) 的縮寫 (contraction)。

　3. 表示 26 個字母 (the alphabet)、數詞 (numerals) 及縮寫字 (abbreviation) 的複數形。

（1） 單數專有名詞 (singular proper noun)、單數普通名詞 (sin-gular common noun) 或特定的代名詞其字尾不是 -s 時，使用「撇號＋s」就可以成為所有格 (possessive case)。

Japan's ancient capital （日本的古都）

China's Great Walls （中國的萬里長城）

Mr. Yoshida's sons and daughters

the boy's younger sister

the elephant's tusk （大象的長牙）

the nation's economy

the city's sewage system （下水道）

today's newspaper　　　　tomorrow's weather

someone else's book　　　　one another's houses

Politics should stop at the water's edge. （政治鬥爭應止於水邊 [內政的紛爭勿扯入外交]。）

What will happen next is anybody's guess. （誰也不知道接下來會發生什麼事。）

It's nobody's business but ours. （這是我們自己的事，與他人無關。）

Global warming is everybody's concern. （全球溫室效應是每個人關心的話題。）

The two leaders agreed to meet in each other's capitals. （兩國領袖已同意在雙方的首都進行會談。）

They were in each other's arms. （他們兩人互相擁抱著。）

（2） 以 -s 結尾的單數普通名詞的所有格，需加上「撇號＋s」。若後面接的單字的首字母為 s 時，則只加撇號。

the stewardess's uniform   the witness's testimony

the stewardess' sister   the witness' success story

（3）　字尾雖不是 -s，但以 [s] 的音結束的單數名詞其後接的單字又是以 s 開頭時，則只加撇號。後接的單字若是 s 以外的字首時，則需加上「撇號＋s」。

for appearance' sake （為了體面）

for conscience' sake （為求心安）

the appearance's cost （花在外表的費用）

my conscience's voice （我良心的聲音）

（4）　以 -s 結尾的單數專有名詞只加撇號。

Achilles' heel （阿基里斯的腳踝；（性格上）唯一的弱點）

Archimedes' principle （阿基米德原理）

Dickens' *Christmas Carol* （狄更斯的「聖誕頌歌」）

Jesus' disciples （耶穌的門徒）

Socrates' view of the soul （蘇格拉底的靈魂觀）

the Court of St. James' (*or* the Court of St. James's) （英國宮廷，引申指英國）

John F. Kennedy's father was the U.S. ambassador to the Court of St. James' before World War II. （第二次世界大戰之前，約翰・甘迺迪的父親曾擔任美國駐英大使。）

注：St. James 的所有格也可寫成 St. James's。

（5）　非以 -s 結尾的複數名詞 (plural noun) 需加上「撇號＋s」。

children's hospital   Children's Day （兒童節）

men's fashion   men's room

women's college   women's rights

（6） 以 -s 結尾的複數名詞及代名詞只需加上撇號。

the boys' choir   the girls' school uniforms

the stewardesses' union

the VIPs' entourage （貴賓們的隨從）

the Joneses' relatives （瓊斯家的親戚）

the Woodses' proud son Tiger （伍茲夫婦引以為傲的兒子——
老虎伍茲）

others' proposals （其他人的提案）

註：敘述之意較所有格的用法強烈時，即使字尾是 -s，也傾
向不加撇號。例如 a teachers college, a writers guide 等
等。這些詞語的意思不是 a college of teachers 和 a guide
of writers，而是 a college for teachers 和 a guide for
writers。即當意思不是表 of 而是 for 時，通常不使用撇
號。

（7） 關於單複數同形的名詞，即使意思是單數，仍可視為複數
看待。

the one deer's antlers （一頭鹿的角）

the two deer's antlers （兩頭鹿的角）

（8） 表示兩人共有的事物時，在第二個人名後加上撇號。

We stayed at John and Bob's summer house for a week. （我們在
約翰和鮑勃共有的避暑山莊停留一個星期。）

Adam and Eve's disobedience led to their expulsion from the Garden of Eden.（由於亞當和夏娃不服從上帝的命令，以至於被驅逐出伊甸園。）

注：若是個別所有時，必須分別加上撇號，被修飾語亦用複數形表示。

We stayed at John's and Bob's summer houses for a week each.

（9） 由兩個以上單字組成的名稱、職務等的所有格，在最後一個單字後面加上「撇號＋s」。

The chairman of the board's business strategy paid off handsomely.（董事長的經營策略非常成功。）

A coalition of civil rights organizations filed a suit alleging that the University of California at Berkeley's new "color-blind" policies discriminate against most minority applicants. — [WP]（民權團體聯合組織主張加州大學柏克萊分校新的「無種族偏見」方針，實際上是在歧視大部分少數民族的應試學生，因此提起訴訟。）

（10） 表示主詞和動詞的縮寫或某些特定片語、詞語的縮寫。

I'm   I can't   I'd   I've   I won't

you're   you'd   you mustn't

he's   he shouldn't   they'd   they won't

o'clock (= of the clock)   will-o'-the-wisp（鬼火）

rock'n'roll (= rock and roll)   'cause (= because)

He was in the class of '95. (= the class of 1995)（他是 1995 年畢

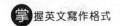

業班的學生。）

（11） 用以省略較長的單字。（特別多用於報紙的新聞標題）

government→ gov't　　　department→ dep't

secretary→ sec'y　　　national→ nat'l

international→ int'l

（12） 也有商店、飯店或雜誌等的名稱會使用「撇號＋s」表示。

The boys gathered at a McDonald's.（青少年們聚集在麥當勞的店門口。）

Macy's（梅西百貨）[美國的大型百貨公司]

Christie's（佳士得）　　　Sotheby's（蘇富比）[兩家都是世界知名的倫敦藝術品、骨董拍賣公司]

Harper's（《哈潑》雜誌）[紐約發行的綜合性雜誌]

（13） 表示數字、字母、單字的複數形時用「撇號＋s」。但是，也有省略撇號的情形。

5's (*or* 5s)　　　9's (*or* 9s)

She is in her mid-50s.（她的年齡約 55 歲。）

She was born in the early 1940s.（她生於 1940 年代初期。）

He got straight A's last year.（他去年拿到全 A 的成績。）

Conservatives are demanding a return to a three-Rs curriculum.（保守派人士正要求恢復讀、寫、算術三門基礎教育課程。）[three Rs = *r*eading, *w*riting and *a*rithmetic]

Mind your p's and q's. *or* Mind your P's and Q's.（留意你的言行舉止。）

But me no but's. (不要找藉口。)

There are many if's in his proposal. (他的提案中有許多但書。)

注：上述最後的兩個例句中，也有只寫 buts 和 ifs 的情形，
即省略了撇號，或亦將 but 和 if 用斜體字寫成 *but*'s 和
if's。

❾ 連字號 (hyphen)　　-

　　將兩個或兩個以上的單字結合成複合字 (compound word)
時使用。又一行中最後一個單字需要斷字換行時，須在行尾加
上連字號表示。

（1）　由於行寬的關係，一行中最後一個單字必須斷字換行時，
　　　要以連字號做為區隔，而連字號必須放在行尾。分割單字時，
　　　應注意勿讓行尾或行首只留下一個字母。

　　注：現今大多數的電腦都備有「行末自動齊行」(justification)
　　　　的功能。而辭典、報紙及其他出版品中，不調整行尾的
　　　　趨勢也益趨明顯，似乎已愈來愈不重視行尾連字號的使
　　　　用了。

（2）　單音節字 (monosyllable *or* one-syllable word) 不分開；而
　　　多音節字 (multisyllable) 分寫兩行時，要以字首 (prefix) 之後、
　　　字尾 (suffix) 之前，或者以音節 (syllable) 為斷字的基準。某些
　　　單字已經含有連字號時，則於連字號處分開。記得必須避免
　　　分割簡短的地名、人名等專有名詞 (proper noun)。

〈單音節字〉

book, head, make, open, safe, talk, tree, etc.

aisle, bread, faith, ghost, judge, quick, etc.

cruise, pounce, shrewd, sluice, throne, etc.

breadth, breathe, cleanse, squeeze, through, etc.

〈多音節字〉（以 - 區分音節）

address	ad-dress
anti-Japanese	an-ti-Jap-a-nese
deregulation	de-reg-u-la-tion
fundamentally	fun-da-men-tal-ly
occurring	oc-cur-ring
possessive	pos-ses-sive
postwar	post-war
preferred	pre-ferred

註：子音 (consonant) 重疊的單字部分，如 ad-dress, oc-cur-ring, pos-ses-sive，可照所示在其間放置連字號即可。此外，英式英語 (BrE) 和美式英語 (AmE) 之間會有微妙的差異（請參照 Part 2「AmE 和 BrE 的拼字法」說明）。

（3） 連字號置於字首 (prefix) 和專有名詞 (proper noun) 之間。

anti-Japanese remarks （反日言論）

neo-Nazism （新納粹主義）

post-Deng Xiaoping China （後鄧小平時代的中國）

pre-Columbus America （哥倫布登陸前的美國）

pro-French regime （親法政權）

Un-American Activities Committee （非美活動委員會）

（4） 首字母為大寫字母的複合字。

We made a U-turn.

He was wearing a T-shirt.

The bus went around an S-shaped bend. （公車行經一處 S 形彎道後離去。）

（5） 連接專有名詞和其後的分詞。

a Nobel Prize-winning author （諾貝爾得獎作家）

an Osaka-based firm （總公司位於大阪的企業）

a U.N.-sponsored environmental conference （聯合國主辦的環境會議）

a Harvard-educated diplomat （哈佛大學畢業的外交官）

（6） 放在修飾名詞的複合修飾語 (compound modifier) 的各個單字之間。

a human-rights activist （人權鬥士）

a shark-infested bay （鯊魚出沒的海灣）

a do-it-yourself kit （DIY 工具組）

an across-the-board surge （[股票等的] 全面性上漲）

a holier-than-thou attitude （自命不凡的態度）

a bases-loaded home run （滿壘全壘打）

an out-of-the-park home run （場外全壘打）

a game-ending home run （再見全壘打）

a come-from-behind victory （反敗為勝）

an environment-friendly product （環保商品）

domestic demand-led growth（內需主導型的成長）

a results-oriented policy（成果導向的政策）

on a case-by-case basis（個案處理）

They reached an out-of-court settlement in the damages suit.（他們在此件損害賠償訴訟案中達成庭外和解。）

After seven years of on-again, off-again reform, Russia seems poised to abandon the reform path altogether.—[WP]（經過 7 年斷斷續續的改革後，俄羅斯似乎決定要完全放棄改革路線。）

注 1：原本以連字號連結的複合字由於經常被使用，所以已有省略連字號變成一個獨立單字的傾向。

anti-Communist→ anticommunist（反共產主義者）

post-Impressionism→ postimpressionism（後印象派）

shock-proof→ shockproof（防震的）

trans-Pacific→ transpacific（橫越太平洋的）

trans-Atlantic→ transatlantic（橫越大西洋的）

注 2：short-distance and long-distance 等片語可結合成 short-and-long-distance。同樣地，「中小企業」也可簡化成 small-and-medium-sized enterprises。這種用法也適用於數字方面。

He received a 10-to-15-year sentence.（他被判 10 到 15 年有期徒刑。）

（7）以 all, ex (= former), pro (= for), self 為字首時，通常要加連字號。

an all-points bulletin（全國通緝令）

an all-weather fighter（全天候型戰鬥機）

his ex-wife (他的前妻)

ex-President George Bush (前總統喬治・布希)

pro-choice (贊成墮胎合法化的)

a pro-lifer (反墮胎的人)

a self-addressed envelope (回郵信封)

a self-winding watch (自動上發條的錶)

注：anti 和 neo 以往也可納入此項規則裡，但是現在除了後面有專有名詞的情形之外，已漸漸不使用連字號。例如：anticlimax (突降法)、antisocial (反社會的)、antiwar (反戰的)、neoclassicism (新古典主義)、neocolonialism (新殖民主義) 等等。另外，pro 和 self 隨著使用頻率的增加，也慢慢地出現省略連字號的傾向，而且已經有報紙和雜誌刊登了諸如 prochoice 和 prolife 等字。

(8) 當字尾為 -ly 的副詞成為複合形容詞的一部分來修飾名詞時，不使用連字號。

a fashionably dressed woman (a well-dressed woman)

a closely guarded secret (a well-kept secret)

a heavily built man (a heavy-set man)

(9) 用於以字母拼出 21 到 99 的數字和分數。

twenty-one   fifty-five   ninety-nine

one-third   two-thirds   three-fifths

He clipped the world record by three-tenths of a second. (他的成績比世界記錄縮短十分之三秒 [0.3 秒]。)

注：one-third 和 a third 意思相同，但後者是由兩個單字組成。

（10）　用於連接數字和單位用語，作為形容詞使用。

the 100-meter dash （100 公尺賽跑）

the 450-seat House of Representatives （450 個席次的眾議院）

a 3,991-meter suspension bridge （3,991 公尺長的吊橋）

a 150,000-ton supertanker （15 萬噸超大型坦克車）

12-mile territorial waters （12 海里的領海）

（11）　多用於表示運動比賽的得分、成績等。

The BayStars defeated the Giants, 6-1.

注：讀法為 six to one 或 six one，和 The BayStars defeated the Giants by a score of six to one. 的意思相同。

The team's 6-1 triumph over the Giants boosted its chances of taking the Central League pennant. （從該隊以 6 比 1 擊敗巨人隊的情形來看，贏得本次中央聯盟的冠軍機會很大。）

Pete Sampras swaggered into the second round, tossing aside the big serves of Marc Goellner for a 6-3, 6-2, 6-2 victory. — [AP]（山普拉斯輕鬆接擊葛爾納強勁的發球，以 6-3、6-2、6-2 獲勝，從容地晉級第二回合比賽。）

Sammy Sosa lined an 0-1 pitch from Brett Tomko (11–11) into the left-field bleachers in the third.—[AP]（第三局，沙米・索沙在球數一好球沒有壞球的情況下，將布萊特・湯可 [11 勝 11 負] 所投出的球打成飛向左外野看臺的平飛全壘打。）

（12）　表示一連串的數字或頁次時要加連字號。

The Nara Period (710-784) saw a flourishing of Buddhist art.（佛教藝術於奈良時代 [西元 710～784 年] 開花結果。）

See pages 60-65 for more details.（詳細內容請參照60～65頁。）

（13） 可用連字號取代 and 和 between 的意思。

Japan-U.S. relations (= relations between Japan and the U.S.)（美日關係）

labor-management relations （勞資關係）

joint Anglo-French undertaking （英法合作企業）

Osaka-Sydney nonstop flight （大阪直飛雪梨班機）

（14） 有些複合名詞本身必須加連字號。

brother-in-law （姊夫；妹夫）

mother-in-law （岳母；婆婆） in-laws （姻親）

lady-in-waiting （宮女；侍女）

forget-me-not （勿忘我草）

love-in-a-mist （黑種草）

（15） 用於表示若干名詞或特殊形容詞等所形成的複合名詞。

the President-elect （[已選出但未就任的] 下任總統）

an ambassador-designate （[已接受任命但尚待議會承認的] 下一任大使）

The hidebound Imperial Household Agency, which handles all royal affairs, quickly taught the princess-to-be to patter a few steps behind her esteemed fiance.—[*Newsweek*] （行事保守、負責皇室所有相關事務的宮內廳 [日本掌管天皇、皇宮事務的機構] 迅速地教導未來的王妃以碎步跟在殿下後面數步的地方。）

（16）　用於合併職業、職位名稱。

secretary-treasurer（祕書兼會計）

singer-songwriter（歌手兼作曲家）

banker-philanthropist（銀行家兼慈善家）

poet-painter（詩人兼畫家）

　注：像「自治大臣兼國家公共安全主委」這樣的官職，不僅名稱長而且又是兼任重要職位，此時經常會使用concurrently 取 代 連 字 號，如 the Home Minister, concurrently Chairman of the National Public Safety Commission。

（17）　加上連字號可避免與拼字相同的單字混淆。

re-collect（再度集合）　　recollect（回憶）

re-count（重新計算）　　recount（敘述）

（18）　加上連字號可避免重複母音或子音時所產生的錯誤發音，使其唸起來像兩個字的發音。

co-op（合作社）　　　　co-opt（選出）

pre-eminent（卓越的）　　pre-empt（搶先取得）

pre-emptive strike（先發制人的攻擊）

re-enlist（重新入伍）

anti-intellectual（反知識分子者）

shell-like（貝殼狀的）

　注1：上述的單字在實際使用時，大多已省略連字號。此外，如 naïve, naïvite, coöperate 的分音符號 ¨ (dieresis) 的蹤影也漸漸消失。

注 2 ：如 anti-imperialism 字首的最後一個字母 i，在接續第
一個字母也是 i 的單字時，必須加上連字號。

anti-intellectualism　(antiwar)

semi-illiterate　(semiconscious)

（19）　特別在美國，使用於人種或民族的起源。

Afro-Americans（非裔美國人）

Irish-Americans（愛爾蘭裔美國人）

Japanese-Americans（日裔美國人）

注：Latin Americans, French Canadians 則不加連字號。

（20）　用於拼寫單字的每一個字母。

The expression "shoo-in" comes from the word "shoo." That is
not the shoe we wear on our foot. It is another word, S-H-O-O.—
[*VOA*]（shoo-in [確定能獲勝的人] 這項說法源自於 shoo。這
和腳上穿的 shoe [鞋] 不一樣，是另一個單字 S-H-O-O。）

（21）　因興奮、害怕而產生結巴的語氣時，可以使用連字號，
並重複字母。

I s-s-see a d-d-dog.（我看…看到一隻…狗…狗。）

10 破折號 (dash)　　　—

　　破折號比逗點表達的分開之意更強烈。即使去掉破折號，
也不會影響句子本身原來的意思。鍵盤上若沒有破折號的按鍵，

則輸入兩次連字號。破折號與前後單字之間不需空格。

注：有些書會建議在破折號的前後各留一個空格。實際上，由於出版社的不同，分為留空格和不留空格兩種。站在出版者的立場，只要發行的刊物統一其中一種方式，自成風格即可。

（1） 用於插入突然想起的詞語或短句等補充說明。

Thus, in most older university communities—mine is one—many faculty members have come to take a rather lofty view of teaching.—[Galbraith]（因此，在大多數具有悠久歷史的大學中——我的母校也是其中之一——許多教職員認為教育是件非常崇高的事。）

I take some pride—very little, mind you—in having started the business from scratch and making them prosper.—[Ward]（我有些驕傲——其實也微不足道——就是這份事業從零開始，而現在做得有聲有色。）

Either crimes of violence, in such cases, are ignored or, if the criminals are brought to trial—this happens very rarely—they are acquitted.—[Steinbeck]（在這種情形下，暴力犯罪不是被忽視，就是即使提出告訴——通常非常少見——犯人也會被無罪釋放。）

（2） 用於說明或引用例證。

The measure must be approved by all five permanent members of the Security Council—Britain, China, France, Russia and the U.S.（此項方案必須由安全理事會的五個常任理事國——英

國、中國、法國、俄國和美國──全體會員國同意方可。）

One can change practically anything these days. The only thing one can't do is make oneself shorter. Some things—noses, body shape, self-esteem—cost an arm and a leg.—[*Independent*] （現今幾乎什麼事情都可以改變。只有一件無法改變的事就是讓人變矮。而舉凡鼻子、身材、自尊心等的改變都需要花費大筆的金錢。）

We had suddenly lost a very special leader whose personal attributes—freshness, youth, humor, style, intelligence, warmth—had made each of us feel renewed pride in the presidency.—[Garrison] （突然之間，我們失去了一位非常特別的領袖，他擁有活力、朝氣、幽默、風度、智慧和熱情等人格特質，這些特質讓我們重新對總統感到自豪。）

（3） 使用於句子的敘述過程中，為表示語氣的突然轉折或強調而預留的間隔。

Washington's assault on export barriers has shocked the sleepy island economies of the Caribbean—and it is ushering in a new era of ill feelings.—[*Newsweek*]（美國政府對出口障礙的譴責，已帶給加勒比海沿岸沈寂的島國經濟非常大的衝擊──並且正進入關係惡化的新時代。）

The time is short—but the agenda is long. Much is to be done—but many are willing.—[JFK] （時間短暫──議題堆積如山。該做的事很多──但也有很多樂於做事的人。）

We are lucky to have a graphics team that can produce such outstanding work week after week—and so, more important, are

our readers.—[*Newsweek*]（我們是何等地幸運擁有這群製圖小組，他們每一週都交出令人讚歎的工作成果——而更重要的是，我們的讀者也很幸運。）

（4） 用於講話者口齒不清或話語的突然中斷時，可以指出其思路的停頓處，也可以使用三個逗點代替。相對於破折號給人的印象為突然間的中斷、結束，逗點會給人慢慢消失的感覺。

"The weather's pretty good, so I'm planning on shooting the—let's see, what's it called?—the Cedar Bridge."—[Waller]（因為天氣很好，所以我想要拍照。嗯…那個叫什麼名字來著？啊，是希得橋！）

"Well, yo—you—well, I mean—if you know beforehand—"—[Christie]（那麼，你…你…我是說…如果你早就知道的話…）

注：第二個例句中，句子的結束是以破折號表示。此時，不以句點結束而以引號標明。

（5） 用於避免表現出明顯的咒罵（swearword）或禁語（taboo word）。

His old friend called him and said, "You poor son of a b—."

注：b— 是 bitch 的省略。因為 son of a bitch 是罵人的話，為避免過分明示而使用破折號表示。這句話另外以 S.O.B. 或 s.o.b. 表示居多。其他例子如：d—n 或 d—（=damn），以及d—d（= damned 過去分詞，讀做 [did]）。

驚嘆號 (exclamation point) ｜ **!**

在英式英語中，稱之為 exclamation mark。由於使用過多的驚嘆號會令人感到寫作技巧不夠純熟，所以寫文章時最好不要太常使用。正式的論文除了引用句外，皆不會使用驚嘆號。

（1）接於感嘆句 (exclamatory sentence) 之後。

How pretty!　　　How wonderful!

How happy the child looked!

What nonsense!　　What a sight!

What a beautiful day it is today!

London, London, London! I was in London! I had been imagining it all my life.—[Baker]（倫敦，倫敦，倫敦，我正在倫敦！我一生夢寐以求的倫敦。）

Let freedom ring from the snowcapped Rockies of Colorado! Let freedom ring from the curvaceous peaks of California! —[King]（讓自由從科羅拉多州白雪皚皚的落磯山脈響徹雲霄！讓自由從加州婀娜多姿的群峰響遍四方！）

注：感嘆句若成為句子中的一部分時，要以句點代替驚嘆號。

She had no idea how happy the child looked.

（2）用於祈使句 (optative sentence)。

God save the Queen! (= May God save the Queen!)（女王萬歲！）

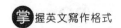

[God Save the Queen 是英國國歌]

Long live the Emperor! (= May the Emperor live long!)

If only you were here!（但願你在我身旁！）

（3） 放在感嘆詞 (interjection) 之後。

Ah!（啊！）　　　　　Bravo!（做得好！）

Gee!（哇！）　　　　　Gosh!（糟了！）

Hello!（哈囉！）　　　Hi!（嗨！）

Hurrah!（萬歲！）　　Ouch!（好痛啊！）

Dear me!（天啊！）　Good for you!（了不起！）

Oh God!　　　　My God!　　　　　Good God!

Heavens!　　　　Good Heavens!　　Jesus!

注1：上例中，Oh God! 以後的詞語都是表現驚訝、忿怒、感嘆或不信任之意，依實際狀況的不同，語意也會隨之改變。

注2：damm, hell 等字雖被當成 swearwords （咒罵） 或 four-letter words （髒話），但這些字也可和驚嘆號一起使用。不過，因為這類的話太過低級下流而被當成 taboo words （禁語），因此使用上需多加留意。

（4） 用於擬聲詞 (onomatopoeia)。

Swish, crack!（咻～碰！）

Splash! The kids leapt into the swimming pool.（撲通一聲，小孩子跳進游泳池裡。）

The door shut with a bang!（門砰地一聲關了起來。）

（5） 用於命令句。

Cool it! （冷靜一點！）

Cut it out! （停！）

Freeze! （[美] 不准動！）

Get out of my sight! （滾開！）

Make it snappy! （趕快！）

Stick it out! （忍著點！）

12 圓括號 (parentheses) ( )

英式英語稱為 brackets。我們一般稱為括號、括弧。由於過度使用此符號可能造成讀者閱讀時的困擾，所以原則上可以用逗點或破折號時，就不要用括號。

（1） 在本文中插入說明、補充的單字、子句、句子時使用。雖然也可以使用破折號，但句意的情境轉折會比用括號來得大。

The hurricane slammed through the tiny village (pop.1,350). （颶風襲擊了這座小村莊 [人口1,350人]。）

When he isn't writing scripts for Jackie Chan, writer/actor Derek Chan (no relation) stays busy operating one of Hong Kong's funkiest curiosity shops.—[*Time*] （當沒有為成龍撰寫劇本時，身兼作家及演員的 Derek Chan [與成龍無親戚關係] 在香港多半忙於經營一家高級骨董店。）

By far the most popular, a series called *Oshin*, ran in 1983-1984. Despite being broadcast at 8:00 A.M. every weekday for about a

year (and repeated during working hours so that salaried men could see it in their offices), at its peak it was being watched by 58 million viewers.—[Emmott]（超人氣的電視連續劇「阿信」，從 1983 年播放至 1984 年。將近一年的時間裡，於星期天以外的每天早上 8 點播放 [這是為了讓上班族能在上班時間在工作場所收看，而於白天重播]，收看人數曾高達 5,800 萬人。）

（2） 表示機構、團體名的縮寫。首先書寫正式名稱，再用（ ）將縮寫字括弧起來。其後再談論到該名稱時，只要用縮寫字表示即可。

The ruling Liberal Democratic Party (LDP) faces stiff competition from the opposition parties headed by the Democratic Party of Japan (DPJ). The LDP suffered a stunning defeat in the 1998 Upper House election.（日本執政黨自民黨正面臨到以民主黨為首的在野黨激烈的競爭。在 1998 年參議院選舉中嚐到嚴重的挫敗。）

（3） 表示詞語的縮寫。和前項用法相同，在出現一次後，其後均可單獨使用縮寫。

The nation's gross domestic product (GDP) registered negative growth for two consecutive years.（該國的國民生產毛額 [GDP] 連續兩年出現負成長。）

The consumer price index (CPI) for January was up 0.2 percentage point from a month before.（1 月份的消費者物價指數 [CPI] 比上個月上揚 0.2 個百分點。）

（4） 用以表示詞語的譯名，或以英文解釋較接近的意思。

Otoko wa Tsuraiyo ("It's Tough Being a Man"), the world's longest-running film series, came to an end in 1997 with the death of actor Kiyoshi Atsumi, who played an itinerant peddler in 48 movies. （日本電影「男人真命苦」[英譯名為 It's Tough Being a Man] 是全世界拍攝最多續集的系列電影 。 一直到 1997 年在 48 部電影中扮演行旅商人的演員渥美清過世後才結束。）

In his last days as Soviet leader, President Mikhail Gorbachev pushed for *glasnost* (openness) and *perestroika* (restructuring). （蘇聯總理戈巴契夫在擔任領導人的最後日子裡，推展國家的資訊公開 [開放] 與經濟改革 [重建]。)[也有像 *glasnost* or openness 是以 or 來取代（ ）的用法]

（5） 表示議員等人的所屬黨派或出身地。

Sens. John F. Kerry (D—Mass.) and Orrin G. Hatch (R—Utah) have little in common, but they share a penchant for legislative activism.—[*WP*] （麻州出身的民主黨參議員凱利和猶他州出身的共和黨參議員哈奇兩人的共通點並不多，但同樣對立法活動非常熱中。）

（6） 用於將度量衡、氣溫等公制 (metric system) 的國際單位換成某特定地區當地讀者容易理解或習慣的說法。

The six-foot-three-inch (192-centimeter) wrestler weighs 310 pounds (180 kilograms). （這位身高 6 呎 3 吋 [192 公分] 的相撲選手體重達 310 磅 [180 公斤]。）

The rocket fell 350-400 km (220-250 miles) from the launch site. (火箭墜落於離發射地點 350～400 公里 [220～250 哩] 的地方。)

The day's high soared to 99 degrees Fahrenheit (37 degrees Celsius). (今天的最高氣溫達到華氏 99 度 [攝氏 37 度]。)

SE England, London: Some sunshine, but becoming cloudier with the chance of a shower. A moderate northeast breeze. Max temp 7-8 C (45-46 F). Tonight, fine and dry with a touch of frost. Min temp−1 C (30 F).—[*Independent*] (英格蘭東南部，倫敦：少許日照，晴後多雲偶陣雨，吹溫煦的東北風。最高氣溫攝氏 37～38 度 [華氏 45～46 度]。夜晚天氣晴朗、乾燥，將會降霜。最低氣溫攝氏零下 1 度 [華氏 30 度]。)

（7） 用於其他貨幣單位表示的金額。

The PC sells for $2,550 (approximately ￥30,600).

The couple bought a small government-subsidized two-bedroom apartment for 1.09 million Hong Kong dollars (140,830 U.S. dollars).—[*AP*] (這對夫婦以 109 萬港幣 [14 萬 830 美元] 買下政府補助的兩房小公寓。)

（8） 表示標號或項目的排序，例如以 (1)、(2)、(3) 或 (A)、(B)、(C) 等標示。

How has the Japanese Miracle been achieved? There were three main factors: (1) hard work and ingenuity; (2) good luck, and (3) a trait which could be politely described as enlightened self-interest, mystically as sacred egoism and more outspokenly

as ruthless selfishness.—[Mikes] （日本的奇蹟是如何產生呢？主要原因有三：(1)工作努力和具創意性；(2)機運佳；(3)民族性——說得好聽一點就是開明的利己主義傾向；說得奧祕一點就是「神聖的利己本位」；說得直截了當就是不顧情理的自私自利。）

(9)　表示出版或上映年代。

In *Syntactic Structures* (1957), Noam Chomsky set out his theory of transformational grammar. （諾姆・喬姆斯基在《句法結構》[1957 年出版] 一書中，闡揚轉換語法的理論。）

Akira Kurosawa's movies include *Rashomon* (1950), *The Seven Samurai* (1954), *Yojimbo* (1961), and *Kagemusha* or *Shadow Warrior* (1980). （導演黑澤明的作品有「羅生門」[1950]、「七武士」[1954]、「大鏢客」[1961] 和「影武者」[1980] 等。）

(10)　用於在句中插入電話號碼、價格等的訊息。而市外電話的區域號碼也以括號表示。

Like any good spy story, Markus Wolf's autobiography, *Man Without a Face* (367 pages. Times Books. $25), offers plenty of thrills.—[*Newsweek*] （如同任何一部好的偵探小說，Markus Wolf 的自傳《沒有臉的男人》[367 頁，時代出版社出版，25 美元] 內容充滿驚悚。）

Call (03) 3456–7890 for details. （詳情請來電 (03) 3456–7890 洽詢。）

(11)　電影或戲劇節目同時出示上場人物和演員的名單時，後

者會顯示於括號內。

Bill and Ben (Belinda Lang and Gary Olsen) head a far-from-average family and endure adventures and nightmares with the help of their children, Jenny and David (Clare Buckfield and John Pickard), and long-time friend and business partner, Rona (Julia Hills).—[*BBC*] （比爾和班 [Belinda Lang 和 Gary Olsen 飾] 擁有破碎的家庭，與孩子珍妮和大衛 [Clare Buckfield 和 John Pickard 飾] 及多年的好友兼工作伙伴蘿娜 [Julia Hills 飾] 一同經歷了許多冒險和恐怖的事。）

（12） 表示人物從出生到死亡及其在職期間、歷史時代等。

About the author of *The Tale of Genji*, Lady Murasaki (*c.* 957–*c.* 1025), we know few facts, but we fortunately still have her diary, which affords us interesting insights into her character. — [Keene]（關於《源氏物語》的作者紫式部 [約西元 957～1025 年]，我們所知不多，但所幸我們仍保有她的日記，可以深入有趣地理解她的性格。）

Britain was at the zenith of its power and prestige during the reign of Queen Victoria (1837-1901). （英國在維多利亞女王在位期間 [西元 1837～1901 年]，國力和威信均達到巔峰。）

（13） 用於表示圖片說明 (photo caption)。

在直述句中插入 (above), (below), (left to right), (front row, third from left) 等詞語，以表示是對特定人物的說明。

（14） 用於表示運動選手的成績。

Hideo Nomo (6-12) was tagged for seven runs and six hits in 2 2/3 innings. （野茂英雄 [6 勝 12 負] 在第二又三分之二局的投球中，被擊出六支安打，並失掉七分。）

Yokozuna Takanohana with 12 wins against one loss is pitted against Sekiwake Kotonishiki (10-3) in the day's final bout. （12 勝 1 負的橫綱貴乃花，將於今日最後一場比賽中迎戰關脇琴錦 [10 勝 3 負]。）

13 方括號 (brackets) [ ]

英式英語稱之為 square brackets，主要用於教科書和論文中。

（1） 為了使引用句和內文容易明瞭，作者或編輯會用方括號插入說明或註解。

It is not in [the U.S.] interest to try to dominate the European councils of decision.—[JFK]（試圖支配歐洲決策會議並不符合 [美國的] 利益。）

In an address to the nation, Clinton claimed he had to strike while the Butler report was hot and because "to initiate military action during Ramadan [coming up over the weekend] would be profoundly offensive to the Muslim world."—[Time]（在對全體國民的演講中，柯林頓總統聲明，他必須趁巴特的報告還令人記憶猶新之際攻擊，並且也因為 [[於本週末開始的] 齋月 [9 月當月之內日出至日落之間禁食] 期間展開軍事行動會對

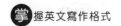

回教世界造成莫大的侮辱」之故。）

（2） 拉丁文 sic (= thus) 用來表示所引用的資料係為原文，並以方括號括起來。為的是告訴讀者該處所用的字不管是否為事實或是語法上有錯誤、錯字，均為原文本身。sic 通常以斜體字表示，即 [*sic*]。

"I am determined to take [*sic*] my utmost effort, at the risk of the Cabinet's life, to bring the Japanese economy to its recovery path within a year or two."—[1998 年 8 月 7 日，小淵首相在國會發表「政策聲明」之譯文]（本人決意要傾全力在一兩年之內讓國內的經濟步上軌道，此事將攸關內閣的命運。）

注：make an effort/make efforts 為慣用的說法，若採用動詞 take，會讓人感到意外，甚至以為 make 被誤植為 take。針對有此疑慮的讀者，出版者特地用 [*sic*] 註明該字為發表的原文，而非印刷錯誤。

14 省略符號 (ellipsis)　　...

以三個句點表示引用句中某一部分（單字、子句或句子）被省略的符號，即稱為省略符號（ellipsis marks 或 suspension points）。

（1） 在引用句中間省略時，要加上三個句點表示。若省略的部分是在句尾時，則包含句尾的句點，共加上四個句點。

Mr. Truman's personal recollections and observations...are the

stuff of which history is made.—[*NYT*]（杜魯門先生個人的回憶與觀察…構成了歷史的本質。）

Fifth. We must reconstruct our relations with the Latin American democracies.... Sixth. We must formulate...a new approach to the Middle East....—[JFK]（第五、我們必須重建與拉丁美洲民主國家的關係。…第六、我們必須樹立…對中東國家的新政策方針…。）

注：要以問號或驚嘆號結束省略之意時，首先先加上三個句點，最後再加上？或！來終止引用。

（2）　省略詩的數行時，則插入一整行句點。

（3）　表示發言的未結束、中斷。

"I'm nobody. Nobody at all.... Leave me alone." She was crying.—[Bernstein]（她哭著說：「我是個沒沒無聞的人，一點出息也沒有。…不要理我。」）

15 斜線 (slash)　　　／

亦稱為 forward slash 或 slant, stroke, [BrE] oblique，也可以稱之為 solidus, virgule。

（1）　表示 or 的意思。

Every person should be free to speak his/her mind.

You can pay by cash/check/credit card.（您可以用現金、支票或

信用卡付款。）

（2） 將兩種物品以斜線連接後，可視為單一物品。

washer/dryer（洗衣乾衣機）

注：亦寫成 washer-dryer 或 washer and dryer。廣告上經常會用 W/D 表示。

（3） 表示 per, a 的意思。

50 meters/second (= 50 meters per second, 50 meters a second)

70 miles/hour (= 70 miles per hour, 70 miles an hour)

（4） 表示 in, of 的意思。

U.S. Forces/Japan (= U.S. Forces in Japan)（駐日美軍）

（5） 表示詞語的省略。

a/c (= account)　　　　　（帳單）

B/L (= bill of lading)　　（提貨單）

c/o (= care of)　　　　　（書信用語「由…轉交」）

M/S (= motor ship)　　　（內燃機船）

L/C (= letter of credit)　（信用狀）

（6） 表示日期。注意美英兩國的月份和日期的順序相反。

8/5/98（美國）=1998 年 8 月 5 日

6/3/99（英國）=1999 年 3 月 6 日

注：請參照 Part 2「數字用法」(3)。

（7） 表示除法 (division) 的分數。一字一字拼出時，分子用基
數 (cardinal number)，分母用序數 (ordinal number) 表示。分子
若為 2 以上，則分母在序數後加 s，並以連字號連接分子與分
母。

1/4	a quarter *or* one fourth
3/4	three quarters *or* three-fourths
1/3	a third *or* one third
2/3	two-thirds
1/2	a half *or* one half
2 1/2 years	two and a half years *or* two years and a half
5 3/5	five and three-fifths
7/10	seven-tenths

The bill fell two votes short of a two-thirds majority required to
make it a law. （此法案必須要三分之二的多數同意才能成為
法律，但尚缺兩票。）

（8） 不直接將詩 (verse) 的原本形式轉記到書寫的內文時，須
加引號，並於詩的分行處以 / 表示，此時，斜線前後各空一格。

My eyes do not discern

as yet that it is fall,

but I can hear it well

in the wind's call

"My eyes do not discern / as yet that it is fall, / but I can hear it
well / in the wind's call."

注：原詩為《古今和歌集》中第四卷藤原敏行的作品。英譯
為 H. H. Honda。

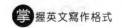

（9） 用於網際網路上的網址。

http://www.whitehouse.gov （美國白宮）

http://www.kantei.go.jp （日本首相官邸）

http://www.oop.gov.tw （中華民國總統府）

http://www.u-tokyo.ac.jp （東京大學）

http://www.kenkyusha.co.jp （研究社）

1999年是MIM，還是MDCCCCLXXXXVIIII?

以羅馬數字 (Roman numerals) 表示「西元 2000 年」時，可以寫做 MM。那麼，1999 年應該如何表示？

據說羅馬數字是在西元前五世紀開始使用，而阿拉伯數字 (Arabic numerals) 是直到十六世紀時才擴展到全世界。阿拉伯數字可以簡單地以 "1999" 表示，但羅馬數字卻不行。標題所提出的問題請容後再做解答，首先先簡單介紹羅馬數字。

羅馬數字由以下七個符號組成，而以這些符號的組合來表現數字的大小。

I = 1,　　　V = 5,　　X = 10,　　　L = 50,

C = 100,　D = 500,　M = 1,000

由於古代羅馬人是用手指數數，因此 II 是 2，III 是 3，IIII 是 4。VI 是 5 + 1 = 6，VII 是 5 + 2 = 7，XV 則

是 10 + 5 = 15。總之，當左側的數字較大時，會以加法方式再加上右側較小的數字計算。

但是，不知從何時起，4 改成以 IV (5 − 1 = 4) 表示。這種新式（且複雜）的表示方法，是以右側較大的數字減掉左側數字的減法方式計算。因此，IX 為 10 − 1 = 9，XIX 為 10 + 10 − 1 = 19，XL為 50 − 10 = 40，XC 為 100 − 10 = 90，CM 為 1,000 − 100 = 900。也就是說，4 和 9 為首的數目均是從右側較大數字減掉左側數字的結果。

有的專家認為從古羅馬的遺跡來看，都可發現上述兩種表示方式，也有學者主張「減法算式」主要是在十九世紀後才開始。在今日，羅馬數字只限定在極少數的場合才會使用，實際生活上和我們沒有多大關係。最後回答標題的問題。

答案是「兩種都正確」。此外，還有另外兩種表示方式。

MIM =（1,000 + 1,000 − 1 = 1999「減法算式」）

MDCCCCLXXXXVIIII（單純的「加法算式」）

MCMXCIX（「減法算式」）

MCMXCVIIII（「減法算式」，但最後的 9 為「加法算式」）

不曉得 1999 年完成的紀念碑及建築物是採用哪一種方法標示？

Part 2

不可不知的用法

1 大寫字 (capitalization)

書寫大寫字 (capitalization *or* uppercasing) 有許多原則，在此謹列記重要原則如下。

（1） 每個句子的句首第一個字母必須大寫。引用句若是完整的句子，其第一個字母亦為大寫。

I said to him, "How do you like Japan?"

"Oh, I like it very much," he replied with great enthusiasm.

> 注 1 ：引用句若非完整的句子，其第一個字母通常要小寫 (lower case)。
>
> He described his success as "totally unexpected."（他說他的成功是「意想不到的。」）

> 注 2 ：引用句若分割為兩個部分時，由於後半部分已非完整的句子，所以其第一個字母不用改成大寫。
>
> "What we must keep in mind," he said, "is that millions of people are facing starvation."（他說道：「我們務必牢記在心的是，目前有數百萬人正處於飢餓當中。」）
>
> "We are living in abundance," he stressed, "at a time when millions of people are on the verge of starvation."（他強調：「當數百萬人瀕臨餓死邊緣時，我們正過著衣食無虞的生活。」）

（2） 專有名詞 (proper noun) 的第一個字母要大寫，由其衍生的形容詞也相同。種類繁多的專有名詞其主要分類如下：

人名：Charlie Chaplin, Romeo, Juliet, Monica Lewinsky, etc. Shakespearian (← Shakespeare), Elizabethan (← Elizabeth), Bostonian (← Boston), etc.

國名及國民：Japan, Japanese; Indonesia, Indonesians; Fiji, Fijians; Cyprus, Cypriots, etc.

語言：Arabic, Chinese, English, French, Russian, Spanish, Mongolian, etc.

地名：San Francisco, Buenos Aires, Cairo, Vienna, the Kuriles （千島群島）, etc.

海洋：the Pacific (Ocean), the Atlantic (Ocean), the Antarctic Ocean （南極海）, the Sea of Japan, etc.

河川：the Chikuma River, the Amazon (River), the Danube （多瑙河）, the Yangtze River （揚子江，長江）, the Nile, the Mississippi, etc.

湖泊：Lake Biwa, Lake Baikal, Lake Michigan, etc.

山、山岳：Mt. Fuji, Chomolungma (Tibetan name for Mt. Everest), the Alps, the Rocky Mountains, etc.

天文、星座：Mercury （水星）, Venus （金星）, Mars （火星）, Ursa Major （the Great Bear 大熊星座）, the Milky Way （銀河）, the Big Dipper （北斗七星）, etc.

> 注：「太陽」寫作 the sun，「月亮」寫作 the moon，皆為小寫字。「地球」通常是用小寫字 the earth，但是在強調與宇宙的對比關係時多寫成 Earth，即變成大寫字且不加冠詞，或者也可以寫成 the planet Earth。

月份、星期：January, December; Sunday, Friday, etc.

節日：New Year's Day, the Fourth of July, Respect for the Aged

Day, Labor Day, Thanksgiving, Christmas, etc.

公共機構：the Diet, the House of Representatives, the Supreme Court, the United Nations, WHO（世界衛生組織）, the Foreign Ministry, etc.

公共團體：the Liberal Democratic Party, the Republican Party, etc.

民間團體、組織：Sony Corp., General Electric, Amnesty International, etc.

宗　教：Buddhism, Christianity, Hinduism, Islam, Judaism, Lamaism, etc.

（3）　書籍、電影、戲劇、電視節目、歌曲、繪畫及雕刻等文藝作品的名稱，除了其中的冠詞 (article)、連接詞 (conjunction) 和介系詞 (preposition) 須小寫外，其餘每一個字的開頭字母必須大寫，通常會以斜體字表示。沒有斜體字型時，以 underline（劃底線）替代。

They were profoundly influenced by Charles Darwin's *On the Origin of Species by Means of Natural Selection.*（他們深受達爾文「物種起源」的理論影響。）

Schindler's List, directed by Steven Spielberg, won seven Academy awards.（史帝芬·史匹柏所導演的電影「辛德勒的名單」榮獲奧斯卡金像獎七項大獎。）

Among Puccini's best known operas is *Madame Butterfly.*（「蝴蝶夫人」是普契尼最有名的歌劇之一。）

注：然而，四個字母以上組成的連接詞、介系詞也有用大寫的情形。也就是如 after, among, between, concerning,

regarding, through, toward, under 等，有時會以大寫字表示。舉例來看：

An Essay Concerning Human Understanding (Book by John Locke)

The Japanese Through American Eyes (Book by Sheila K. Johnson)

Changing Japanese Attitudes Toward Modernization (Book edited by Marius B. Jansen)

（4） 表示作品、產品。

The museum has a large collection of Picassos and Rembrandts.

He has purchased a Honda Accord.

He shows off his Rolex.

（5） 置於人名前的職稱、職業名。

President John F. Kennedy of the United States

Mayor Ichiro Yamada of Osaka

注：職稱名若為補語或和人名分開單獨使用時，通常為小寫。

The president was assassinated in Dallas, Texas, on November 22, 1963.（總統於 1963 年 11 月 22 日在德州達拉斯遭到暗殺。）

Ichiro Yamada was reelected mayor of Osaka last week.

（6） 根據方位指示的地區位置名以大寫字表示。若單純指示方向則為小寫字。

He was born in the Northeast of China.（中國東北部）

George Wallace was from the South.（美國南部）

We faced a strong northeast wind.（強烈的東北風 [方向]）

Kobe is about 30 kilometers west of Osaka.（神戶位於大阪西方約 30 公里處 [方向]。）

（7）　用於表示地區的通稱。

Political developments in the Middle East deserve close attention.（中東的政治情勢發展值得密切關注。）

The Lake District in northwest England is known for its scenic beauty.（英國西北部的湖泊區因其明媚的風光而遠近馳名。）

The Big Apple is a popular name for New York City.（大蘋果是紐約市的通稱。）

The U.S. Department of State is sometimes referred to as Foggy Bottom.（美國國務院有時被稱為霧谷。）

（8）　表示特定的時代、歷史事件。

Jura, the Jurassic（侏羅紀）　　the Paleozoic（古生代）

the Dark Ages（黑暗時代）　　the Middle Ages（中世紀）

the Renaissance（文藝復興時期）

the Tokugawa Period（德川時代）

the Exodus（逃離埃及）

the Diaspora（猶太人大流散）

the Holocaust（[第二次世界大戰時] 納粹對猶太人的大屠殺）

the Great Depression（[1929 年始於美國的] 世界經濟大恐慌）

World War II (= the Second World War)（第二次世界大戰）

（9） 表示重要文件、重要活動或獎項名。

The freedom of religion is guaranteed by the Constitution.（宗教信仰的自由受憲法保障。）

Japan and South Korea will co-host the 2002 World Cup.（日本和南韓將共同舉辦 2002 年的世界盃 [足球] 大賽。）

Kenzaburo Oe received the Nobel Prize for Literature in 1995.（大江健三郎榮獲 1995 年諾貝爾文學獎。）

Akira Kurosawa won the top prize at the 1951 Venice Film Festival for *Rashomon*.（黑澤明的電影「羅生門」榮獲 1951 年威尼斯影展的最高獎項。）

（10） 表示紀念碑、歷史性建築物或遺跡。

the Golden Pavilion （[日本] 金閣寺），the Katsura Detached Palace （[日本] 桂離宮）

the Forbidden City （[中國清朝皇宮] 紫禁城）

Angkor Wat （[東埔寨的佛教遺址] 吳哥窟）

Taj Mahal（[十七世紀印度的蒙兀兒帝國汗王為其愛妃所建的陵墓] 泰姬瑪哈陵）

the Dome of the Rock （[耶路撒冷的回教聖地] 岩石圓頂）

the Wailing wall （[耶路撒冷的猶太教聖地] 哭牆）

the Leaning Tower of Pisa （[義大利] 比薩斜塔）

the Valley of the Kings （[古埃及] 王家之谷）

（11） 表示學位。

He is working for an MA degree. (= master of arts)（碩士學位）

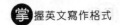

She earned a Ph.D. from Oxford. (= doctor of philosophy)（博士學位）

（12）　出現在一連串數字前的名詞，其第一個字母要大寫。

Article 9, Paragraph 2 of the Constitution（憲法第 9 條第 2 項）

Open your textbook to Page 25.

We will meet in Room 5.

注：於憲法、條約及其他重要法規裡，以阿拉伯數字 (Arabic numerals) 表示的情形會比以羅馬數字 (Roman numerals) 如 ARTICLE IX（第 9 條）表示的情形來得多（參照 Part 2「數字用法」(12)、(13)）。

（13）　表示親屬的稱謂。

I remember Mother moving busily in the kitchen as Father sat reading the newspaper.（我回想起父親坐著看報紙，而母親在廚房裡忙進忙出的景象。）

注：以大寫字書寫親人的稱謂是一種親密關係的展現，此時不加 my。

② 斜體字 (italics)

　　印刷字體包括常見的羅馬正體鉛字 (roman) 和斜體字 (italics)。沒有斜體字的打字機，則在羅馬字體底下加劃底線代替。

（1） 表示書籍、報紙、雜誌、電影、戲劇、音樂作品、電視節目等的標題。但諸如刊載在一本書裡的短篇故事或報章雜誌的個別報導的標題，則不使用斜體字，而是用引號（請參照 Part 1「引號」說明）。

The only Western book of which I am reminded in reading *The Tale of Genji* is Marcel Proust's *A la Recherche du Temps Perdu.*—[Keene]（當我閱讀《源氏物語》時，唯一聯想到的西洋小說是馬塞爾•普魯斯特的《追憶似水年華》。）

The splitting of an infinitive, a once sacrosanct no-no frowned upon by grammarians across the English-speaking world, has been condoned by the authoritative *New Oxford Dictionary of English.*—[Time]（以往英語系的國家裡，文法學者均厭惡分割不定詞，視此為神聖不可侵犯之禁忌。而今，最具權威性的《新牛津辭典》已不再嚴格約束。）

He left the taxi and returned burdened with the early Sunday editions of *The New York Times, Daily News,* and *Post.*—[Hailey]（他下計程車，手裡抱著星期天的《紐約時報》、《每日新聞》和《郵報》回來。）

She [my mother] was desperately poor, but she found money to buy me magazine subscriptions to *Boy's Life* and *American Boy,* and later *The Atlantic Monthly* and *Harper's.*—[Baker]（她 [我的母親] 雖然很窮，但仍籌錢替我訂閱《男孩生活》、《美國男孩》和之後的《亞特蘭大月刊》、《哈潑》雜誌。）

In Hong Kong, *Godzilla* opened better than *Titanic.*—[Time]（在香港，電影「酷斯拉」的票房比「鐵達尼號」還好。）

For me, it's not Christmas without the *Messiah.*—[Kuralt]（對我

而言，在聖誕節不聽 [韓德爾的]「彌賽亞」就不算過聖誕節。）
Leonard Bernstein's *West Side Story* burst onto Broadway in
September 1957. This contemporary version of Shakespeare's
Romeo and Juliet, set among warring New York gangs, caught
the imagination of a new generation of theatre-goers. —
[*BBC*]（雷納多・伯恩斯坦的《西城故事》於 1957 年 9 月光
榮躍上百老匯舞臺。此齣翻自莎翁名作《羅密歐與茱麗葉》
的現代版，描寫紐約市兩個對立的不良少年幫派，深深抓住
了新世代音樂劇迷的心。）

（2） 船舶、軍艦的名稱也多以斜體字表示。

The *Titanic* struck an iceberg on the night of April 14-15, 1912
and sank on its maiden voyage from Southampton, England, to
New York City.（鐵達尼號在從英國的南安普敦港開往紐約的
處女航中，於 1912 年 4 月 14 日的夜晚到 15 日的凌晨撞上冰
山，沈入海底。）

'I can put together a task force of destroyers, frigates, landing
craft, support vessels. It will be led by the aircraft carriers HMS
Hermes and HMS *Invincible*. It can be ready to leave in
forty-eight hours.' —[Thatcher]（我可以組織一個由驅逐艦、護
航艦、登陸艇、補給艦所組成的機動部隊。它們將由航空母
艦赫美斯號和無敵號帶領。機動部隊可在 48 小時內整裝出
發。）[HMS = Her Majesty's Ship]

（3） 表示外文字彙或外來語。若能更進一步以英文解釋其意
的話，更能幫助讀者閱讀、理解。

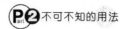

In Japan, they are known as *shinjinrui*, which can roughly be translated as "new humans."—[Emmott]

Japanese employees who serve abroad for a very long period of time have virtually no chance to rise to the very top positions in their firms, for they are considered a bit too *gaijin kusai* (contaminated by foreignness).—[Vogel]（長期在海外工作的日本公司的員工，實際上在回國後很難爬升到最高職位，因為他們會被認為有些「外國人的腥味」[受到洋化的污染]。）

My mother was very sad that I was going, and kept saying she was sorry I had to miss the traditional Chinese New Year breakfast which her camp was going to serve: *tang-yuan*, round dumplings, symbolizing family union.—[Chang]（母親對於我的即將離去感到非常難過，並不停地說，她為我不能吃到她的收容所為正月新年的早餐所準備的湯圓 [象徵一家團圓的圓麵粉糰] 而感到惋惜。）[*tang-yuan* 為中文「湯圓」的音譯]

"*Pardon monsieur*, I should like to speak to you for one moment." — [Maugham] （對不起，我想佔用你一點時間。）[*Pardon monsieur* 是法文，代表 Pardon me, Mister 的意思]

Centuries ago, Portuguese explorers named this whole Amazon complex *O Rio Mar*, The River Sea.—[Hailey]（幾世紀前，葡萄牙探險家們將亞馬遜河流域命名為 *O Rio Mar*，也就是「河海」的意思。）[*O Rio Mar* 是葡萄牙語]

（4） 表示強調。

Life *is* a game, boy. Life *is* a game that one plays according to

the rules.—[Salinger]（孩子，人生就好像遊戲——是一場依循規則的遊戲。）

At eighty-five, when he no longer had *the somethings to look forward to* daily, his health deteriorated rapidly.—[Ward]（他在85歲時失去了一些每日可引頸企盼的事，以至於身體狀況急速惡化。）

"*Now* is the time to make real the promise of Democracy. *Now* is the time to rise from the dark and desolate valley of segregation to the sunlit path of racial justice. *Now* is the time to open the doors of opportunity to all of God's children."—[King]（現在正是實現民主主義承諾的時刻。現在正是擺脫種族隔離的黑暗荒涼山谷、邁向陽光普照而沒有種族歧視的光明大道的時刻。現在正是為所有神的子民打開機會之窗的時刻。）

（5） 表示某單字雖屬於句子中的一部分，卻不具任何意思，只單純做為單字使用。

Many words end in *y*, which is silent. （許多單字以 y 結尾，不發音。）

Old people, especially, will say *noo* for "new" and when they say *bar*, *storm* or *yard*, the *r* is not sounded.—[*BBC: The Story of English*]（特別是老年人，常將 new 發音成 noo，而且在發 bar, storm 或 yard 的音時，r 會變成無聲。）

3 拼字的基本法則

　　若將單字拼錯 (misspelling) 了，不僅很丟臉，還會因為意思不明確，容易招致誤解。對於單字的正確拼法沒有把握時，記得查辭典。又當寫好一篇文章時，亦須反覆閱讀，以注意拼字上有無錯誤，這是最基本且重要的寫作態度。關於英文單字的拼字，在此僅就其基本規則做列舉式的說明。但要明白有規則就會有例外，所以也要留意例外的情形。另外，關於名詞的複數形請參照本書「複數形」說明。

（1）　首先 be, have 以外動詞的第三人稱單數形 (third-person singular form)，一般是加上 -s。但是，字尾若是 -ch, -sh, -o, -x 時則加上 -es；字尾為 -y 時，-y 改成 -i 並加上 -es。

+ s	He walks to school.
	She reads the newspaper every day.
	（其他：begin, call, demand, enter, give, etc.）
-ch → + es	He teaches English at high school.
	（其他：clinch, pinch, poach, preach, etc.）
-sh → + es	She washes her hair twice a day.
	（其他：blush, crush, punish, push, smash, etc.）
-o → + es	She goes to school every day.
	（其他：do, forgo, overdo, torpedo, etc.）
-x → + es	He fixes his own shoes.
	（其他：annex, fax, flex, reflex, relax, etc.）
-y → i + es	She studies English and Chinese in school.
	（其他：clarify, cry, fly, testify, try, etc.）

注：字尾 -y 的前面是母音時，只要加 -s 即可。

　　annoy → annoys　　　buy → buys　　　delay → delays

obey → obeys   play → plays   say → says

（2）　規則動詞 (regular verb) 的過去式和過去分詞，採原形加
-ed 的形式。字尾為 -e 時則加 -d，以 -y 為結尾的單字則將 -y
改成 -i 再加 -ed。

	現在式	過去式	過去分詞
+ ed	abandon	abandon*ed*	abandon*ed*
	hand	hand*ed*	hand*ed*
	work	work*ed*	work*ed*
+ d	announc*e*	announc*ed*	announc*ed*
	star*e*	star*ed*	star*ed*
y → i + ed	cry	cr*ied*	cr*ied*
	accompany	accompan*ied*	accompan*ied*

注：字尾 -y 的前面是母音時，只要加 -ed 即可。

ann*oy*　　　　annoy*ed*　　　　annoy*ed*

pl*ay*　　　　play*ed*　　　　play*ed*

（3）　p, b, m 之前的子音，原則上多為 m，而不是 n。

p　　impatient, impossible, impractical, impulse, jump,
　　　slump, umpire, etc.

b　　ambitious, bomb, combination, member, mumble,
　　　timber, umbrella, etc.

m　　immigration, immoral, immediate, imminent, immortal,
　　　immune, etc.

注 1：有些字首為 in-, un- 的單字並不適用上述原則。

in-　inpour, input; inborn, inbreeding; inmate, inmost,

etc.

un-　unpaid, unpopular; unbelievable, unbecoming; unmarried, unmoved, etc.

注 2：balance 有 imbalance (imbalanced) 和 unbalance (un-balanced) 兩個接否定形式字首的單字。兩者都解釋為 lack of balance 的意思。但前者如 trade imbalance（貿易不均衡），是用於表示兩個或兩個以上的人或物之間無法取得平衡；後者則多意指精神狀態的不穩定。

（4）　重音 (stress) 落在單字的最後，又重音節的母音是短母音時，在接 -ing, -ed, -er [-or] 時，須重複字尾的子音。

hit　　→ hitting, hitter

plan　　→ planning, planned, planner

run　　→ running, runner

stun　　→ stunning, stunned, stunner

admit　→ admitting, admitted

begin　→ beginning, beginner

incur　→ incurring, incurred

permit → permitting, permitted, permitter

refer　→ referring, referred（名詞為 reference，重音移到前面的 re-）

submit → submitting, submitted, submitter

注 1：下列的單字不適用上述規則。

gossip → gossiping, gossiped, gossiper [因為重音在第一個母音 o 上]

suffer → suffering, suffered, sufferer [因為重音在第一

個母音 u 上]

torment → tormenting, tormented, tormenter/tormentor
[重音雖然在第二個母音 e 上，但是其後有兩個子音 (n, t)]

注2：英式英語中，如 travel 這類重音不在最後音節的單字，字尾也會重複加 l，但美式英語不須重複。

(AmE)　travel 　→ traveling, traveled, traveler

(BrE)　travel 　→ travelling, travelled, traveller

quarrel → quarrelling, quarrelled, quarreller

bedevil → bedevilling, bedevilled

shrivel → shrivelling, shrivelled

snivel 　→ snivelling, snivelled, sniveller

（5） 英式英語中，下列動詞的重音雖不在最後音節，仍要重複最後面的子音。美式英語中也有重複的情形（斜線前為英式英語 BrE，斜線後為美式英語 AmE）。

handicap → handicapping, handicapped, handicapper　（BrE 和 AmE 共通）

hiccup 　→ hiccupping/hiccuping, hiccupped/hiccuped

kidnap 　→ kidnapping/kidnaping, kidnapped/kidnaped, kidnapper/kidnaper

program → programming/programing, programmed/programed, programmer/programer

worship 　→ worshipping/worshiping, worshipped/worshiped, worshipper/worshiper

（6） 單字最後字母的 e 為無聲子音 (silent)，在接續以母音為
始的字尾 (suffix) 如 -ing, -ed, -er, -or, -able 時，e 會消失。

arrange → arranging, arranged, arranger

change → changing, changed, changer （changeable 另參照註
解）

live → living, lived, livable

prove → proving, proved, provable

score → scoring, scored, scorer

注 1 ：字尾的第一個字母是 a 或 o 時，仍可常見到無聲子音
e 的存在。特別是 e 之前為 c 或 g 時，最常發生。

change + able → changeable

notice + able → noticeable

trace + able → traceable

courage + ous → courageous

(fame + ous → famous)

outrage + ous → outrageous

（例外：prestige + ous → prestigious）

注意上例中，每一個 c 都不唸做 [k] 而唸做 [s]，不唸
做 [g] 而唸做 [dʒ]，是一些發音較不費力的弱子音
(lenis)。

注 2 ：為了避免和類似的單字混淆，有時也會保留無聲子音
e。

die → dying dye → dyeing

sing → singing singe → singeing

（7） 當最後字母的 -e 為無聲子音，要接以子音為始的字尾時，

大部分會將 e 保留。

amaze + ment → amazement

require + ment → requirement

hope + ful → hopeful

use + ful → useful

pure + ly → purely

sure + ly → surely

注：也有不保留 -e 的情形。

argue + ment → argument

judge + ment → judgment

nine + th → ninth

true + th → truth

awe + ful → awful

due + ly → duly

true + ly → truly

（8）　單字的最後字母為 -y，在接另一個字尾前，會將 -y 改成 -i；但是接 -ing 之前，則保留原本的 -y。

carry → carries, carried, carrier; carrying

fly → flies, flier; flying

hurry → hurries, hurried; hurrying

marry → marries, married, marriage; marrying

try → tries, tried, trial; trying

注：一個音節的形容詞，其單字最後的 -y 通常會保留。

dry → dryness, dryly（動詞為 dries, dried, drying，比較級、最高級為 drier, driest。）

shy → shyness, shyly （動詞為 shies, shied, shying，比較級、最高級為 shyer/shier, shyest/shiest。）

sly → slyness, slyly （比較級、最高級為 slyer/slier, slyest/sliest。）

wry → wryness, wryly （動詞為 wries, wried, wrying，比較級、最高級為 wrier, wriest。）

（9） 當最後字母為 -y 的形容詞要變成比較級 (-er) 和最高級 (-est) 時，若 y 的前面是子音，則將 y 改成 i，若為母音時則不變。

子音 + y	foggy	foggier	foggiest
	happy	happier	happiest
	lucky	luckier	luckiest
母音 + y	coy	coyer	coyest
	gay	gayer	gayest
	gray	grayer	grayest

（10） 形容詞加 -ly 變成副詞時，必須根據形容詞字尾做拼字變化。舉出其中較為重要的例子做說明：

形容詞→副詞

'-ic' → '-ically'	automatic	→ automatically
	economic	→ economically
	tragic	→ tragically
	（例外：public → publicly）	
'-le' → '-ly'	gentle	→ gently
	subtle	→ subtly

（例外：supple → supplely, whole → wholly）

'-y' → '-ily'　　　easy　　　→ easily

happy　　　→ happily

lucky　　　→ luckily

（例外：y 的前面為母音時則為 -ly）

c*oy*　　　→ coyly

g*ay*　　　→ gayly/gaily

（11）　單字的最後一個字母為 -c [k]，在連接 -ing, -ed, -y 時，須加上 k。

panic　→ panicking, panicked, panicky

picnic → picnicking, picnicked

traffic → trafficking, trafficked

（12）　以 -ie [aɪ] 為最後字母的單字在連接 -ing 時，要將 ie 改成 y。

die → dying　　　lie → lying

tie → tying　　　vie → vying

4　AmE 和 BrE 的拼字法

關於美式英語 (AmE) 和英式英語 (BrE) 之間的差異，姑且不論兩者發音上有何不同，先就下列三點看出兩者明顯的差別。

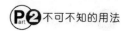

1. 單字拼法不同

2. 事物名稱不同

[AmE]	[BrE]	[AmE]	[BrE]
elevator	lift	railroad	railway
gasoline	petrol	truck	lorry
hood	bonnet	vacuum cleaner	hoover

3. 語法不同

[AmE]	[BrE]
the first floor（第一個樓層）	（二樓）
He is in hospital.	He is in the hospital.
It was the worst flood in 20 years.	It was the worst flood for 20 years.

　　因本書性質限定在第一點上，故只針對該點討論。整體而言，加拿大人書寫的英文接近 AmE；另一方面，在澳洲、紐西蘭、南非共和國甚至印度、巴基斯坦等國，則是 BrE 拼字法較具優勢。

　　關於拼字法 (spelling)，雖然現今 AmE 和 BrE 的差異有日漸縮小的傾向，但還是可從下列提出的各點看出明顯的不同。另外，雖然美式和英式英語不會因拼字法的不同而造成理解上的阻力，但是同一本書為維持同一風格，還是應該避免混用。

（1）　AmE 中，以 -l 為最後一個字母、由兩個音節以上組成且重音不在最後音節上的單字，在接 -ing 等字尾時，不會重複 "l"。BrE 則必須重複 "l"。

　　[AmE]　　　　　[BrE]

traveling	travelling
traveled	travelled
traveler	traveller

（其他：barrel, quarrel, etc.）

重音落在最後音節時，不管 AmE 或 BrE，兩者都要重複最後的子音字母 (consonant)。

acquit	acquitting	acquitted	acquitter
admit	admitting	admitted	admittance
compel	compelling	compelled	
confer	conferring	conferred	conferree/conferee
control	controlling	controlled	controller
occur	occurring	occurred	occurrence
omit	omitting	omitted	omission
permit	permitting	permitted	permission
prefer	preferring	preferred	(preference)
regret	regretting	regretted	regrettable

（其他：commit, concur, defer, equip, expel, incur, propel, quit, refer, submit, etc.）

注：preference 之所以例外是因其重音移到最前面的 e。

（2） 在 AmE 中，有幾個動詞的最後一個子音字母會重複，但在 BrE 中並沒有重複。不過，兩者在接 -ing, -ed 時，拼字法相同。

[AmE]	[BrE]	[AmE/BrE]	
appall	appal	appalling	appalled
distill	distil	distilling	distilled

enroll	enrol	enrolling	enrolled
extoll	extol	extolling	extolled
fulfill	fulfil	fulfilling	fulfilled
install	instal	installing	installed

注：上述單字的名詞形，例如 fulfillment, fulfilment 在 AmE 和 BrE 之間的差別微乎其微，有愈來愈多的辭典不做區分。

（3） skill 的形容詞有 skillful (AmE) 和 skilful (BrE) 兩種。副詞有 skillfully (AmE), skilfully (BrE) 兩種。另一個形容詞 skilled 在 AmE 和 BrE 中，拼法是一樣。

（4） 單字在 AmE 中，只有一個子音，但在 BrE 中，有兩個子音。例如：

[AmE]	[BrE]
woolen	woollen
jewelry, jeweler	jewellry, jeweller
jeweled, jeweling	jewelled, jewelling
program, programer	programme, programmer
programed, programing	programmed, programming
tranquilize, tranquilizer	tranquillize, tranquilizer

（5） AmE 和 BrE 拼字法的差異還可歸納出幾個主要類別。區分如下：

[AmE]	[BrE]	[AmE]	[BrE]	
-or	-our	color	colour	（色彩）

		favor	favour	（贊成）
		glamor	glamour	（魅力）
		honor	honour	（名譽）
		humor	humour	（幽默感）
		labor	labour	（勞動）
		valor	valour	（勇氣）
-er	-re	center	centre	（中心）
		fiber	fibre	（纖維）
		meter	metre	（計量器）
		somber	sombre	（憂鬱的）
		specter	spectre	（幽靈）
		theater	theatre	（劇場）
-se	-ce	defense	defence	（防衛）
		license	licence	（許可）
		offense	offence	（犯罪，攻擊）
		pretense	pretence	（假裝）
		vise	vice	（虎頭鉗）
		(practice	practise)	（實行）
-ize	-ise	analyze	analyse	（分析）
		memorize	memorise	（背熟）
		nationalize	nationalise	（使國有化）
		polarize	polarise	（使極化）
		realize	realise	（領悟）

注：英國也有逐漸使用 -ize 的傾向。

-ization	-isation	civilization	civilisation	（文明）
		naturalization	naturalisation	（歸化）

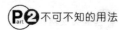

-e	-ae, -oe	esthetics	aesthetics	（美學）
		ameba	amoeba	（變形蟲）
		archeology	archaeology	（考古學）
		diarrhea	diarrhoea	（腹瀉）
		encyclopedia	encyclopaedia	（百科全書）
		gynecology	gynaecology	（婦科醫學）
		medieval	mediaeval	（中世紀的）
-ol	-oul	mold	mould	（鑄模；黴）
		molder	moulder	（腐爛）
		moldy	mouldy	（發霉的）
		molt	moult	（脫皮）
		smolder	smoulder	（悶燒）
-t	-tte	cigaret	cigarette	（香菸）
		omelet	omelette	（煎蛋捲）
-og	-ogue	catalog	catalogue	（目錄）
		dialog	dialogue	（對話）

注：有些辭典會同時收錄 prologue 和 prolog 兩字，不過 prolog 不如 catalog 和 dialog 被廣泛熟知。

（6） 其他。和以上的例子一樣，下面的單字在 AmE 和 BrE 中，亦沒有絕對的差異。

[AmE]	[BrE]	
aluminum	aluminium	（鋁）
ax	axe	（斧頭）
behoove	behove	（有必要）
check	cheque	（支票）

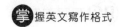

dependence	dependance	（依賴）
draft	draught	（草稿）
furor	furore	（狂熱）
glycerin	glycerine	（甘油）
gray	grey	（灰色）
jail	gaol	（監獄）
mustache	moustache	（鬍鬚）
naught	nought	（零）
plow	plough	（犁）
pajamas	pyjamas	（睡衣褲）
skepticism	scepticism	（懷疑論）
specialty	speciality	（專長）
tire	tyre	（輪胎）

5 可數名詞的複數形 (plural)

可以用一個、兩個數事物的名詞，稱作可數名詞 (countable noun)。大多數只要在單字最後加 -s 即可成為複數形 (plural)。但是，也有不少名詞必須使用其他方法表示。此外，單複數同形的名詞有時須改成不規則複數形。

（1） 字尾加 -s。

book → books　　girl → girls　　pocket → pockets
river → rivers　　ship → ships　　tree → trees

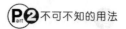

（2） 字尾為 -ch, -s, -sh, -ss, -x, -zz 時加 -es，為 -z 時加 -zes。

church → churches	search → searches	torch → torches
bonus → bonuses	bus → buses	lens → lenses
clash → clashes	dish → dishes	wish → wishes
boss → bosses	glass → glasses	mass → masses
box → boxes	fax → faxes	fox → foxes
buzz → buzzes	fez → fezzes	quiz → quizzes

注：當 ch 發成 [k] 時加 -s。

       monarch → monarchs   stomach → stomachs

       mach → machs   oligarch → oligarchs

（3） 字尾為 -f 時，分成只加 -s 和將 f 變成 v 之後加 -es 兩種方式。

-s   belief → beliefs   chief → chiefs

              proof → proofs   roof → roofs

              （其他：cliff, fief, gulf, etc.）

(f → v) -es   leaf → leaves   shelf → shelves

              thief → thieves

              （其他：calf, elf, half, loaf, self, sheaf, etc.）

注：handkerchief 有 handkerchiefs 和 handkerchieves 兩個複

    數形。其他如 beef, hoof, scarf, turf, wharf 等同樣也有兩

    個複數形。

（4） 字尾為 -fe 時，同樣也有只加 -s 和將 f 改成 v 之後再加

    -es 兩種方式。

-s   carafe → carafes   safe → safes

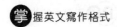

                    strafe → strafes

(f → v) -es   knife → knives   life → lives

                    wife → wives

（5）　若字尾音發 [f]，則加 -s。

-ph [f]   nymph   → nymphs

               paragraph   → paragraphs

               photograph   → photographs

               triumph   → triumphs

-gh [f]   cough → coughs   laugh → laughs

               rough → roughs   trough → troughs

（6）　單字最後字母為 o，且前一個字母為母音時加 -s。若前一
　　　個字母為子音，大多數也是加 -s，但也有加 -es 的情形。單字
　　　最後為 -oo 時，則只加 -s。

[母音]   o   embryo → embryos

                           folio → folios   radio → radios

                           （其他：curio, patio, scenario, solo,

                           studio, trio, etc.）

[子音]   o   -s   memo → memos   photo → photos

                           piano → pianos   solo → solos

                           （其他：alto, combo, concerto, libido,

                           limbo, pimento, tango, taro, torso,

                           tuxedo, two, etc.）

              -es   echo → echoes   hero → heroes

                           potato → potatoes   veto → vetoes

（其他：embargo, jingo, negro, tomato, torpedo, etc.）

-oo　-s　　kangaroo → kangaroos

taboo → taboos　　zoo → zoos

（其他：cuckoo, hoodoo, loo, shampoo, tattoo, etc.）

注：有些單字可以同時接 -s 或 -es。

buffalo → buffalos, buffaloes

tobacco → tobaccos, tobaccoes

（其他：cargo, dado, domino, flamingo, fresco, ghetto, halo, indigo, innuendo, manifesto, memento, motto, stucco, tornado, volcano, zero, etc.）

（7）　最後字母為 -y，且之前字母是子音或 qu 時，將 y 改成 i 再加 -es。若是母音則直接加 -s。

-y → ies　　body → bodies　　city → cities

spy → spies　　story → stories

（其他：army, bully, cry, economy, party, purgatory, sky, soliloquy, etc.）

-s　　boy → boys　　day → days

key → keys　　toy → toys

（其他：buoy, decoy, donkey, monkey, play, ploy, pulley, turkey, valley, etc.）

注：專有名詞則不受此項原則限制。

the two Germanys（東西德）

the Kennedys（甘迺迪夫婦；甘迺迪家族）

（8） 單複數同形的名詞。此類名詞大多數為動物和魚的名稱。

aircraft（飛機）, barracks（兵營）, corps（軍團）, crossroads（十字路口）, means（手段）, offspring（子孫）, series（系列）, shambles（混亂場面）, species（種類）, etc.

（單數） An aircraft was sighted heading north over the mountain.（有人目擊到 1 架飛機越過山頭向北邊飛去。）

（複數） Ten hostile aircraft were shot down in the aerial battle.（10 架敵機在一次空戰中被擊落。）

注：corps 為單數時發 [kɔr] 的音，複數時發 [kɔrz] 的音。

動物：antelope（羚羊）, caribou（北美馴鹿）, deer（鹿）, elk（駝鹿）, grouse（松雞）, moose（麋）, reindeer（馴鹿）, sheep（羊）, etc.

魚： carp（鯉魚）, cod（鱈魚）, goldfish（金魚）, halibut（大比目魚）, mullet（鯔魚）, salmon（鮭魚）, shellfish（甲殼水生動物）, trout（鱒魚）, whitebait（銀魚）, etc.

注 1：上述的每個名詞都可以做集合名詞用。例如：

Deer are herbivorous.（鹿是草食性動物。）

至於單數名詞的例句：

A male deer with a magnificent antler crossed a shady path ahead of us in Nara Park.（在奈良公園裡，一隻頭上頂著漂亮鹿角的公鹿橫越過我們前方的林蔭步道。）

注 2：前面所列名詞除了 sheep, whitebait 之外，均有加 -s 或

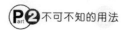
　　-es 的複數形，做為集合名詞以外的複數形使用。

（9）　經常以複數形出現的名詞。以單數形無法充分表現本身
　　　之意的單字，如服飾、裝飾品及道具之類：

breeches（馬褲）, briefs（短內褲）, clothes（衣服）, glasses（眼
鏡）, jeans（牛仔褲）, pajamas（睡衣褲）, pants（褲子）, shorts（寬
鬆運動短褲）, spectacles（眼鏡）, stockings（長襪）,
sunglasses（太陽眼鏡）, suspenders（吊褲帶）, tights（緊身
衣）, trousers（褲子）, etc.

bellows（風箱）, binoculars（雙筒望遠鏡）, chopsticks（筷
子）, fetters（腳鐐）, gallows（絞刑臺）, handcuffs（手銬）,
pincers（鉗子）, pliers（鑷子）, scales（比例尺）, scissors（剪
刀）, stilts（高蹺）, tongs（火鉗）, etc.

身體部位：bowels（腸）, entrails（內臟）, genitals（生殖器）,
　　　　　gums（牙齦）, guts（內臟）, sideburns（鬢角）,
　　　　　whiskers（髯）, etc.

疾病、感覺：cramps（抽筋）, chills（寒慄）, convulsions（痙
攣）, creeps（毛骨悚然的感覺）, diabetes（糖尿病）, dismals（憂
鬱）, dumps（憂鬱）, jitters（神經過敏）, jives（胡扯）,
hysterics（歇斯底里）, measles（痲疹）, mumps（腮腺炎）,
rabies（狂犬病）, rickets（軟骨病）, shivers（顫抖）, sniffles
（鼻塞）, snuffles（鼻塞）, staggers（蹣跚）, etc.

遊戲：billiards（撞球）, bowls（保齡球）, cards（撲克牌）,
charades（猜字謎遊戲）, darts（射鏢遊戲）, marbles（彈
珠）, etc.

建築物、場所：eaves（屋簷）, headquarters（總部）, links（高爾夫球場）, premises（房宅）, works（工廠）, etc.

學術領域：economics（經濟學）, ethics（倫理學）, linguistics（語言學）, logistics（後勤學）, mathematics（數學）, physics（物理學）, politics（政治學）, robotics（機器人學）, statistics（統計學）, etc.

注：若做為學術上某一領域之意時，要採單數形，其後的動詞也隨之變化。但是表示的若是活動或性質之意時，則要採複數形，同樣地，動詞亦要隨之變化。

Statistics is the science of assembling, classifying and analyzing facts or data.（統計學是一門收集事實或資料並加以分類、分析的學問。）

Statistics show that Japan's population will fall bellow the 100 million mark in 2051.（根據統計，西元 2051 年的日本人口將不超過 1 億人。）

其他：ashes（遺骸）, belongings（財產）, customs（關稅）, dregs（渣滓）, drinkables（飲料）, droppings（鳥獸的糞便）, eatables（食物）, environs（近郊）, futures（期貨）, goods（動產；貨品）, letters（文學）, perishables（生鮮食品）, remains（遺骨）, riches（財富）, savings（儲蓄）, summons（傳票）, trappings（裝飾）, valuables（貴重物品）, victuals（食品）

（10） 雖然是複數形，但在意思上被視同單數看待的名詞。

The news was received with great interest.（這則報導引起很大的關注。）

其他如 measles, mumps 等疾病以及上述學術類等名稱亦同。

（11）　複合名詞的複數形。

在單字最後加上 -s 的情況最多。

language school	→ language schools （語言學校）
travel agent	→ travel agents （旅行社）

在複合名詞的主要單字後加上 -s 或 -es。

bird of passage	→ birds of passage （候鳥）
brother-in-law	→ brothers-in-law （姊夫；妹夫）
commander-in-chief	→ commanders-in-chief （總司令）
dropper-in	→ droppers-in （不速之客）
hand-me-down	→ hand-me-downs （別人穿過的舊衣服）
lady-in-waiting	→ ladies-in-waiting （宮女；侍女）
looker-on	→ lookers-on （觀看者）
passer-by	→ passers-by （行人）
sergeant-at-arms	→ sergeants-at-arms （守衛）

（12）　縮寫字、數字或文字的複數形要加 -s 或者 -'s。

MP (= member of Parliament) → MPs

VIP (= very important person) → VIPs

He wants to master the ABCs of golf.

She is in her late 60s.

The airline has a fleet of 20 Boeing 747s. （這家航空公司擁有 20 架波音 747 飛機。）

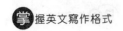

He got five A's and four B's last semester.

The word "small" has two l's. ("small" 這個單字有兩個 l。)

Mind your p's and q's. (注意你的禮節。)

His proposal is full of "ifs." (他的提案中有許多但書。)

注：只有 A, B, p, q 這類一個字母的名詞，會加 -'s 表示複數形。其他的大多只加 -s。

（13）　專有名詞的複數形。用於表示夫婦、兄弟姊妹或一家人，以及表示地區時使用。

大部分會在專有名詞前加上定冠詞 (the) 和在單字最後加上 -s。

　　Kimuras → the Kimuras （木村夫婦）

　　the Clintons, the Lincolns, the Rockefellers

　　the Americas （美洲）

　　the two Koreas （南北韓）

以 -es, -z 結尾的專有名詞則加 -es。

　　Charles → the Charleses

　　Jones → the Joneses

　　Gonzalez → the Gonzalezes

以 -y 結尾的專有名詞，即使前一個字母是子音也加 -s。

　　the Kellys, the Kennedys

　　　（例外：the Rockies → the Rocky Mountains）

（14）　受拉丁文及其他外國語文的語言規則影響所產生的複數形。這類單字有些本身即帶有英文的複數形 (-s)。

-us → -i　　　　alumnus → alumni （同班同學）

focus → foci (*or* focuses) （焦點）

radius → radii (*or* radiuses) （半徑）

stimulus → stimuli （刺激）, etc.

-us → （其他） corpus → corpora （全集）

genius → geniuses （天才）

genus → genera (*or* genuses) （[生物的] 屬）, etc.

-um → -a　aquarium → aquaria (*or* aquariums) （水族館）

conundrum → conundra (*or* conundrums)（謎語）

curriculum → curricula (*or* curriculums) （課程）

mausoleum → mausolea (*or* mausoleums) （陵墓）

medium → media (*or* mediums) （媒體）

memorandum → memoranda (*or* memorandums) （備忘錄）, etc.

注：agenda（議程）雖然是 agendumn 的複數形，但在今日都被視為單數形，而另以 agendas 做為其複數形。同樣地，data（資料）也是 datum 的複數形，但口語英語都視之為單數，動詞也隨之用單數形表示。

-a → -ae　alumna → alumnae （女校友）

formula → formulae (*or* formulas) （公式）

larva → larvae （幼蟲）

vertebra → vertebrae (*or* vertebras) （脊椎骨）, etc.

-is → -es　analysis → analyses （分析）

basis → bases （基礎）

catalysis → catalyses （催化作用）

（其他：crisis （危機），dialysis （透析），hypothesis （假設），neurosis （精神官能症），oasis（綠洲），paralysis（麻痺），parenthesis（圓括號），etc.）

-ix, -ex → -ices   appendix → appendices (*or* appendixes)（附錄）

index → indices (*or* indexes)（指標）

matrix → matrices (*or* matrixes)（母體；字模）

vortex → vortices (*or* vortexes)（旋渦），etc.

-on （希臘文字尾）→ -a   criterion → criteria (*or* criterions)（基準）

phenomenon → phenomena (*or* phenomenons)（現象），etc.

-eau （法文字尾）→ -aux   bureau → bureaux (*or* bureaus)（局，處）

trousseau → trousseaux (*or* trousseaus)（嫁妝），etc.

（15） 名詞的不規則複數形。

child → children,   grandchild → grandchildren

brother → brothers, brethren

man → men,   cameraman → cameramen,

chairman → chairmen,

Congressman → Congressmen,

Dutchman → Dutchmen,

Englishman → Englishmen, postman → postmen, etc.

woman → women, chairwoman → chairwomen,

Congresswoman → Congresswomen,

Englishwoman → Englishwomen, etc.

foot → feet, goose → geese（鵝）,

louse → lice（蝨子）, mouse → mice（老鼠）,

ox → oxen（牛）, tooth → teeth（牙齒）

（16） 國民的單數及複數。

單複數同形（字尾為 -ese, -s）。

The group included one Japanese and three Americans.（這個團體裡有一名日本人和三名美國人。）

Ten Japanese were aboard the plane.（飛機上有十名日本人。）

國名	國民（單數）	國民（複數）
China	Chinese	Chinese
Congo	Congolese	Congolese
Lebanon	Lebanese	Lebanese
Malta	Maltese	Maltese
Nepal	Nepalese	Nepalese
Portugal	Portuguese	Portuguese
Senegal	Senegalese	Senegalese
Togo	Togolese	Togolese
Vietnam	Vietnamese	Vietnamese
Seychelles	Seychellois	Seychellois
Switzerland	Swiss	Swiss

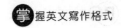

單數加上 -s 即變複數。

國名	國民（單數）	國民（複數）
Argentina	Argentine	Argentines
Australia	Australian	Australians
Bangladesh	Bangladeshi	Bangladeshis
Belarus	Belarusian	Belarusians
Brunei	Bruneian	Bruneians
Cyprus	Cypriot	Cypriots
Czech Republic	Czech	Czechs
Denmark	Dane	Danes
Egypt	Egyptian	Egyptians
Fiji	Fijian	Fijians
Finland	Finn	Finns
Germany	German	Germans
Haiti	Haitian	Haitians
Israel	Israeli	Israelis
Jamaica	Jamaican	Jamaicans
Jordan	Jordanian	Jordanians
Kwait	Kwaiti	Kwaitis
Laos	Laotian	Laotians
Liechtenstein	Liechtensteiner	Liechtensteiners
Luxembourg	Luxembourger	Luxembourgers
Mexico	Mexican	Mexicans
Norway	Norwegian	Norwegians
Pakistan	Pakistani	Pakistanis

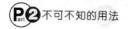

Peru	Peruvian	Peruvians
Philippines	Filipino	Filipinos
Poland	Pole	Poles
Singapore	Singaporean	Singaporeans
Spain	Spaniard	Spaniards
Sri Lanka	Sri Lankan	Sri Lankans
Sweden	Swede	Swedes
Thailand	Thai	Thais
	Thailander	Thailanders
United Kingdom	Briton	Britons
United States	American	Americans
Yemen	Yemenite	Yemenites
Yugoslavia	Yugoslav	Yugoslavs
Zambia	Zambian	Zambians
Zimbabwe	Zimbabwean	Zimbabweans

注 1 ：統稱全體國民時以 the＋國民（複數）的形式較為常見，並同樣做複數使用。例如，日本人的統稱為 the Japanese，德國人的統稱為 the Germans，菲律賓人的統稱為 the Filipinos。但也有例外的情形，主要有以下幾項：

國家	國民的統稱
France	the French
Ireland	the Irish
Netherlands	the Dutch
Spain	the Spanish
United Kingdom	the British

注 2 ：英國的正式名稱為 the United Kingdom of Great Britain and Northern Ireland（大不列顛及北愛爾蘭聯合王國），省略寫法為 the United Kingdom 或 the U.K.。英國人的名稱則為 a Briton/Britons/the British。大不列顛現在是由 England（英格蘭）, Scotland（蘇格蘭）和 Wales（威爾斯）等地方所組成。由於以前是個別的國家，所以至今各地方的人仍然存在著彼此是不同民族的獨立意識。例如今日舉行運動比賽時，大多會以不同的國家來看待。居民的稱呼如下：

地方	單數	複數	統稱
England	Englishman	Englishmen	the English
Scotland	Scot	Scots	the Scots
Wales	Welshman	Welshmen	the Welsh

6 數字用法

（1）　除非特殊情形，否則一般都使用阿拉伯數字（Arabic numerals）。在句子中的數目 1 到 9 以拼成英文單字為原則，10 以上則用數字（figures）表示。不單是基數（cardinal number）如此，序數（ordinal number）也一樣。

Our team consisted of three women and five men.（我們這一隊是由三個女人和五個男人所組成。）

The high school has 350 boys and 390 girls.（這所中學的男學生為 350 人，女學生為 390 人。）

He finished first in the 10-man race and his younger brother

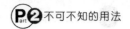

came in third.（他在十人的比賽中獲得冠軍，他的弟弟則是第三名。）

Pope John Paul II is the 264th leader of the Roman Catholic Church.（若望・保祿二世是羅馬天主教會第 264 任教宗。）

（2）　表示年齡或長度、幅度、厚度等度量單位時，要用數字。此時，9 以下也可以用數字顯示。

He was 15 years old when he published his first novel.（他在 15 歲時出版了第一本小說。）

She has a 6-year-old daughter.（她有一個 6 歲大的女兒。）

The table is 2 meters long, 1.5 meters wide and 1.2 meters high.（這張桌子長 2 公尺、寬 1.5 公尺、高 1.2 公尺。）

Search vessels combed an area 50 miles by 30 miles.（搜查艇在 1,500 海里的海域上徹底搜尋。）

（3）　日期、時間一般也使用數字。

She was born on August 5, 1985.

The Hikari super express left Tokyo at 8 a.m.

We boarded the 9:30 p.m. flight for London.（我們搭乘晚間 9 點 30 分的飛機前往倫敦。）

注：在英國，特別將日期寫成序數，如 She was born on August 5th, 1985. 或 She was born on the fifth of August, 1985.。

除此之外，用數字表示年、月、日時，美式和英式在寫法順序上會有不同。

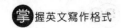

美式　8/5/85（月／日／年　August 5, 1985）

英式　8/5/85（日／月／年　May 8, 1985）

（4）句子中出現好幾個數目時，即使是 9 以下，大部分也用數字表示。而統計及圖表說明等，也是常用數字表示 9 以下的數目。

Thus, the tanka is a poem in 31 syllables, arranged in lines of 5, 7, 5, 7 and 7 syllables.—[Keene]（因此，短歌為 31 個音節的詩，每一行音節數以 5, 7, 5, 7, 7 的方式排列。）

The Nikkei average closed at 13,706, down 3 points from last Friday.（日經指數平均收盤價為 1 萬 3,706 日圓，比上星期五跌了 3 點。）

（5）原則上在句首不使用數字，必須拼成單字。不過，西元年可以數字的形式放在句首。

Three persons were killed in the fire.

Ninety-five guests were invited to the party.

2000 will be a crucial year for millions of computers which cannot distinguish between 2000 and 1900.（由於數百萬臺電腦無法區別 2000 年和 1900 年，所以西元 2000 年對電腦的發展將是很重要的一年。）

= The year 2000 will be crucial for millions of computer.... [相較之下，這樣的寫法比較平穩]

注：又例如將「598人」寫成 Five hundred [and] ninety-eight people 並放在句首時，會變得難以閱讀，而且也很佔空間。若改成「大約 600 人」的概數 (round number) 形式，

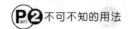

即在句首用 about, approximately, some 再接數字的話會
比較好。或者用 A total of ～ 等詞語將數字從句首抽離
也是一種方法,甚至也可以從句法結構上著手。總之,
儘量不要將數字放在句首。

About 600 people were made homeless in the fire. (大約有
600 人因這場火災而無家可歸。)

A total of 598 people lost their homes in the fire.

The fire left 598 people without homes.

(6) 數目大的數字,會在每三個位數前以逗點分開,使人容易
閱讀、理解。

123	(one hundred [and] twenty-three)
1,234	(one thousand two hundred thirty-four)
12,345	(twelve thousand three hundred forty-five)
123,456	(one hundred twenty-three thousand four hundred fifty-six)
1,234,567	(one million ～)
12,345,678	(twelve million ～)
123,456,789	(one hundred twenty-three million ～)
1,234,567,890	(one billion ～ [美]; one thousand two hundred thirty-four million ～ [英])

(7) 以下雖為四位數數字,但卻不在三位數前加上逗點。

西元年:Japan's population will peak in [the year] 2010. (日本
人口將於西元 2010 年達到極限。)

地　址：The White House is at 1600 Pennsylvania Avenue, Washington, D.C.

電話、傳真號碼：Call us toll-free at 03–3331–1113.（免付費電話）

　　Fax this coupon to + 44 171 240 4899.

注：44 是代表英國的國際電話國碼 [country code]（日本是 81，臺灣是 886）。171 是倫敦的區域號碼 [area code]。240 4899 是對方的電話號碼 [telephone number]。書面上，區域號碼會用 ( ) 括起來，即如 (03), (171) 一樣。

郵遞區號 (postal code/zip code)：100–0014

UTC（= Universal Time Coordinated，簡稱 Universal Time，譯為世界協調時間，等同 GMT [= Greenwich Mean Time] 之意，GMT 即為全世界通用的格林威治標準時間）、地區時間等：

　　The interview will be broadcast live from the White House at 1500 UTC.

書刊的頁碼

（8）　西元前（B.C. 或 BC）的年代也不在每三個位數前以逗點分開，而西元後（A.D. 或 AD）通常不使用四位數記年。須注意 B.C. 和 A.D. 的位置。（請參閱 Coffee Break「西曆與美國曆」）

2500 B.C.　100 B.C.　[B.C. 在年代後]

A.D. 50　　A.D. 100　[A.D. 在年代前]

Cleopatra [69-30 B.C.] was the last ruler in the dynasty founded by Ptolemy I in 323 B.C.（克麗奧佩脫拉 [西元前 69 ～ 30 年]

是西元前 323 年由托勒密一世建立埃及王朝的最後一位女王。）

The Jomon period was followed by the Yayoi period (ca 300 B.C.–ca A.D. 300). （繩文時代之後是彌生時代 [約西元前 300 年到西元 300 年左右]。）

注：B.C. 是 before Christ 的省略。A.D. 是拉丁文 Anno Domini 的省略，表示是 in the year of our Lord, in the year since the birth of Christ 的意思。

（9） 溫度、經緯度、距離、比賽的時間，以及得票數、得分、百分比等都用數字。

The temperature shot up to 33 degrees Celsius. （氣溫上升至攝氏 33 度。）

The yacht gave its position at 158 degrees 20 minutes west longitude and 21 degrees 45 minutes north latitude. （這艘遊艇的位置在北緯 21 度 45 分，西經 158 度 20 分。） [圖表上則顯示 158°20′W, 21°45′N，若顯示的單位及於秒 (second) 則變成 158°20′35″W]

In the 1988 Seoul Olympic Games, Griffith Joyner set a world record in the 100-meter dash in 10:54. （1998 年漢城奧運，葛瑞菲絲以 10 秒 54 刷新了 100 公尺短跑的世界記錄。）

The Security Council approved the resolution with a vote of 10 to 3 with two abstentions. （安全理事會以贊成票 10 票對反對票 3 票，以及棄權 2 票通過了該項決議案。）

The Yokohama BayStars defeated the Seibu Lions, 4-2, in the four-of-seven-game Japan Series. （在日本七戰四勝的系列賽

中，橫濱海灣之星隊以 4 勝 2 負擊敗了西武獅子隊，奪得冠軍。）

The candidate won 56 percent of the vote. （該名候選人在此次選戰中贏得了 56% 的選票。）

（10）　以下情形亦使用數字。

戲劇場次：Act 1, Scene 2 （第 1 幕第 2 場）

科目編號：English 2, French 1

書籍章節：Chapter 2

房間號碼：Room 5

（11）　在句中的分數 (fraction) 若是 1 以下時，要拼出單字來。若為 1 以上，則最好換成小數點。

A two-thirds majority is needed for the bill to clear the legislature.（法案在議會需要有三分之二以上的人贊成才能通過立法。）

He bettered the record by three tenths of a second. （他以十分之三秒刷新了記錄。）

Prices went up by 2.3 percent last year. （去年物價上漲了 2.3%。）

The trade surplus last year totaled $15.56 billion. （去年的貿易順差總額達 155 億 6,000 萬美元。）

注：使用 million, billion 時，小數點只用在一位數或二位數前。另外，切記 million 和 billion 不能同時使用，不可以把 $15.56 billion 寫成 $15 billion and $560 million。

（12） 羅馬數字 (Roman numerals) 多用來表示皇族、羅馬教皇或有來歷的家族繼承人。同時也可以使用於戰爭、遊艇、名馬等，或者奧林匹克和其他定期且持續性召開的國際會議等名稱上。甚至用來表示雕刻在紀念碑或建築物基石上的完成年，以及時鐘的刻度盤上。

Queen Elizabeth II (II = the second) （伊莉莎白女王二世）

King George VI (VI = the sixth) （喬治六世） [Queen Elizabeth II 之父]

Pope John Paul II （教宗若望・保祿二世）

Louis XIV (XIV = the fourteenth) （路易十四）

the XIV Dalai Lama （達賴喇嘛十四世）

World War II (II = two) （或是 the Second World War）

the XXVIIth Olympiad （第 27 屆奧林匹克運動會）

the Shamrock IV; the Canonero II （遊艇名）

注：有關羅馬數字的詳細介紹，請參閱 Coffee Break 「1999 年是 MIM 還是 MDCCCLXXXXVIIII？」。

（13） 條約、法律中最高的章節或條款多用羅馬數字，其次的條項則用阿拉伯數字表示。

日本憲法：CHAPTER IV （第四章）, Article 41 （第 41 條）

美國憲法：ARTICLE XXII（第二十二條）, Section 2（第 2 項）

聯合國憲章：CHAPTER XIX （第十九章）, Article 111 （第 111 條）

美日安保條約：ARTICLE VI （第六條）

（14） 現在還可見到某些學術性的書籍中，卷首的 contents（目次）、preface（序言）、acknowledgments（感謝詞）及卷尾的 index（索引）上的頁次會以羅馬數字表示，而內文的頁次則習慣使用阿拉伯數字。不過，現今書籍的冊數、章節有愈來愈少用羅馬數字的傾向。

 縮寫字和頭字語

現今英文報紙的縮寫字（abbreviation）似乎已多到氾濫的程度。特別是大標題（headline），記者若不用縮寫字似乎就沒辦法下筆。新的技術、研究、商品和組織機構也加速了使用縮寫字的潮流。這是由於英文單字本身大多很長，所以自然而然只能仰賴縮寫字和頭字語（acronym）了。

大部分利用電子郵件（e-mail）的人會經常使用縮寫字，而各行各業也在個別的領域裡發展出專門使用的縮寫字，也有不少縮寫字已經跨越自身的領域，廣為一般人使用。

但是，除了某些領域的同業人士或者同好者之間的交談之外，在寫文章給不特定的多數人時，要切記避免在不自覺的情況下使用縮寫字。若使用對方無法了解的縮寫字，不僅不能傳達訊息，還會讓對方感到不愉快。

使用縮寫字、頭字語時，一定要留意只能使用廣泛通用的文字，或者是對方容易理解的字。除此之外，在一篇文章中要多次書寫同一個詞語時，可先將欲省略的單字或片語完整拼出，並在其後用圓括號（parentheses）顯示縮寫字，以後即可重複使用該縮寫字。如果只是出現一次的詞語，就不需要刻意使用縮

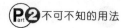
寫字。舉例說明如下：

　　The ruling Liberal Democratic Party (LDP) and the Liberal Party (LP) have agreed to form a coalition aimed at achieving greater political stability needed to pull the nation out of its prolonged economic crisis. The agreement has ended five years of often hostile relations between the two conservative parties after Ichiro Ozawa, LP chairman, bolted the LDP over policy differences. （自民黨和自由黨為了擺脫我國［日本］長期的經濟危機，達成了以實現政治安定為目標的聯合協議。這項協議顯示出從自由黨黨魁小澤一郎因政策分歧脫離自民黨以來，兩個保守政黨之間長達五年的對立關係已宣告結束。）

　　過去為明確表示是縮寫字，習慣上會在後面加上句點。但由於字數長的縮寫字和首字語的急速增加，以及為了節省在每個字後面加句點的時間及空間，漸漸傾向於將句點省略。

　　此外，美國和英國在關於句點的使用上也有不同。例如：美國的報章雜誌在 the U.S. (= United States), the U.K. (= United Kingdom), the U.N. (= United Nations) 的每個大寫字後面習慣加上句點。這些加上句點的縮寫字用在像 the U.S. Government 的形容詞用法時也一樣。相對地，英國的報章雜誌在 the US, the UN 後不加句點，大多只有 the U.K. 時才加句點。另外在美國，如 UNESCO, UNICEF 是全以大寫字 (all caps) 表示，而在英國則大部分只將首字母以大寫顯示，如 Unesco, Unicef。

◆縮寫字可分為以下三類：

（1）　省略詞語的一部分。

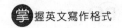

人名前的敬稱、抬頭的縮寫。

Mr. Frank Sinatra　　　　(Mr. = mister)

Mrs. Tina Turner　　　　 (Mrs. = mistress)

Dr. Benny Hill　　　　　 (Dr. = doctor)

the Rev. Jessie Jackson　　(Rev. = reverend)

Sen. Edward Kennedy　　 (Sen. = senator)

Adm. John Dewey　　　　(Adm. = admiral)

注：在英國，對於由第一個字母和最後一個字母構成的縮寫字，大多傾向於將象徵縮寫字的句點省略。

　　Mr Joe Casey　　　　　Dr Nick Hornby

日期、數字的縮寫。

She was born on Jan. 31, 1980.　(Jan. = January)

The king died circa 350 B.C.　(B.C. = before Christ)（國王於西元前 350 年駕崩。）

注：月份和星期通常會拼出完整單字。如上述之月份和日期一前一後出現時，才會使用月份的縮寫字。不過，通常也只限於 Jan., Feb., Aug., Sep., Oct., Nov., Dec. 等，至於 March, April, May, June, July 並不縮寫。若使用受限於版面篇幅不足的圖表時，便可如 Mar, Apr, May, Jun, Jul 將各月份省略句點並縮寫成三個字母。星期通常也要完整拼出單字，但是用於圖表上時，同樣可以先省略各單字的句點並縮寫成三個字母，如 Sun, Mon, Tue, Wed, Thu, Fri, Sat。

住址、方向的縮寫。

The White House is at 1600 Pennsylvania Ave., Washington,

D.C. (Ave. = avenue, D.C. = District of Columbia)

PO Box 76S, Bush House, Strand, London, WC2B. (PO = post office, WC = west central)

注：地址中沒有伴隨門牌號碼的字，如 avenue, street 等通常要完整拼出單字。

單位的縮寫。

C (= Celsius 攝氏), F (= Fahrenheit 華氏), g (= gram), m (= meter), km (= kilometer), w (= watts), etc.

由單字前幾個字母組成的縮寫字。

asst. (= assistant), dept. (= department), cont. (= continued), org. (= organization), pref. (= prefecture), vol. (= volume), etc.

省略數個字母的縮寫字。

HQ (= headquarters), Jr. (= junior), ms (= manuscript 原稿), P.S. (= postscript 附註), Sgt. (= sergeant 中士), Sr. (= senior), etc.

專門用語的縮寫字。 此類縮寫字有不少比縮寫前的原本名稱還廣為人知。

CFCs (= chlorofluorocarbons 含氯氟烴), hPa (= hectopascal 百帕 [氣壓的單位]), TB (= tuberculosis 肺結核)

（2）用於省略兩個以上的單字。此種縮寫字的範圍遍及國際組織、政治、經濟、社會團體、技術、學問、流行等各個領域，佔了今日一般常用縮寫字的絕大部分，甚至大多數會比原本的正式名稱還廣為人知，AIDS 即是一例。以下僅列出較為常見的詞彙供參考。

國際組織：

APEC（= Asia-Pacific Economic Cooperation 亞太經濟合作會議）

EU（= European Union 歐洲聯盟）

OPEC（= Organization of Petroleum Exporting Countries 石油輸出國家組織）

U.N.（= United Nations 聯合國）

UNESCO（= United Nations Educational, Scientific and Cultural Organization 聯合國教育科學暨文化組織）

政治、行政：

DPJ（= Democratic Party of Japan [日本] 民主黨）

FBI（= Federal Bureau of Investigation [美國] 聯邦調查局）

LDP（= Liberal Democratic Party [日本] 自民黨）

MITI（= Ministry of International Trade and Industry [日本] 通產省）[相當於我國經濟部]

MP（= Member of Parliament [英國] 國會議員）

經濟：

BOJ（= Bank of Japan 日本銀行）

CEO（= chief executive officer 總裁）

GM（= General Motors Corp [美國] 通用汽車）[世界最大汽車公司]

JETRO（= Japan External Trade Organization 日本貿易振興會）

NYSE（= New York Stock Exchange 紐約證券交易所）

媒體：

AFP（= Agence France Press 法新社）

AP（= Associated Press [美國] 美聯社）

BBC（= British Broadcasting Corporation 英國廣播公司）

CNN（= Cable News Network [美國] 有線電視新聞網）

NHK（= Nihon Hoso Kyokai = Japan Broadcasting Corporation 日本放送協會）

太空：

EPIRB（= emergency position indication radio beacon 緊急位置無線電示標）

LM（= lunar module 登月艇）

NASA（= National Aeronautics and Space Administration [美國] 太空總署）

NASDA（= National Space Development Agency of Japan 日本太空總署）

武器、裁軍：

AAM（= air-to-air missile 空對空飛彈）

CTBT（= Comprehensive Test Ban Treaty 全面禁止核子實驗條約）

ICBM（= intercontinental ballistic missile 洲際彈道飛彈）

NPT（= Nuclear Nonproliferation Treaty 防止核子擴散條約）

SALT（= Strategic Arms Limitation Treaty 限制戰略武器談判）

醫學、醫療：

AIDS（= acquired immune deficiency syndrome 愛滋病，後天免疫不全症候群）

CJD（= Creutzfeldt-Jakob disease 類似「狂牛症」的疾病）

HIV（= human immunodeficiency virus 人體免疫缺損病毒）

MRI（= magnetic resonance imaging 核磁共振顯像）

SMON disease（= subacute myelo-optico-neuropathy 亞急性脊髓視神經症）

電腦、網際網路：

CD-ROM（= compact disc read-only memory 光碟唯讀記憶體）

CPU（= central processing unit 中央處理機）

FAQ（= frequently asked questions 常見問題）

LAN（= local area network 局部 [企業內] 區域網路）

WWW（= World Wide Web 全球資訊網）

原有的縮寫字：

a.k.a.（= also known as 又名，亦稱）

asap（= as soon as possible 儘快）

COD（= cash on delivery/collect on delivery 貨到付款）

FY（= fiscal year 會計年度）

FYI（= for your information 僅供參考）

（3） 句子的縮寫。

IMHO（= in my humble opinion 以我謙遜的意見）[e-mail 用語]

IOU（= I owe you. 借條）

KISS（= keep it short and simple 保持簡潔）[e-mail 用語]

PTO（= please turn over 接次頁）

RSVP（= repondez s'il vous plait (Fr.) = please reply 敬請答覆）

[請帖用語]

◆**頭字語 (acronym)：**

　　通常由三個以上的首字母組成，不可以字母個別發音，必須視為一個單字來發音。例如 APEC 不可唸成 [e-pi-i-si]，而是視 apec 為一個單字，唸成 [`epɛk]。同樣地，UNESCO 不是唸成 [ju-ɛn-i-ɛs-si-o]，而是唸成 [ju`nɛsko]。上述 (2) 所列舉的縮寫字當中，AIDS, OPEC, JETRO, NASA, NASDA, SALT 等都是頭字語。

　　若縮寫字原本的正式名稱帶有定冠詞 (definite article) the，當一成為頭字語之後，通常都會省略該定冠詞。例如 NASA 的正式名稱為 the National Aeronautics and Space Administration，將其省略成 NASA 時，並不加 the。相反地，FBI 和 LDP 因為不是頭字語，所以即使變成縮寫字，也和正式名稱 the Federal Bureau of Investigation, the Liberal Democratic Party 一樣要加 the，即 the FBI, the LDP。

　　有些名稱變成頭字語後，字仍顯得很長，於是出現和一般專有名詞一樣，只有首字母為大寫的傾向。英國的報紙上即曾出現上述提到的 Unesco 及 Unicef (聯合國兒童基金會) 形式的頭字語，但是這聯合國兩大機構本身仍堅持全部使用大寫字 UNESCO, UNICEF 表示。

　　注：英國的報章雜誌大多以 Uno 代表聯合國。這是由 United Nations Organization 各個單字的第一個字母組成並且將首字母加以大寫的結果，發成 [`juno] 的音。須留意 Uno 和縮寫字 the U.N.不同，前面並不接 the。

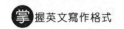

Coffee Break

西曆和「美國曆」

　　二十世紀已接近尾聲，即將開始另一個新的世紀和新的 millennium（千禧年）。說到「年」，我們都能靈活地使用「1999 年」、「平成 11 年」和「民國 88 年」等以表示年份。

　　「1999 年」當然是指「西元 1999 年」，不過在英文中，只用 1999 或 the year 1999 來表示即可。然而，在比較重視形式的文件或宣言（是指以基督教為主要宗教的國家所公布）上，會使用 the year of our Lord 1999 表示。

　　美國總統經常發表 Proclamation（聲明書）。由於是注重格式的公文，所以具有很莊嚴慎重的寫作風格。以下將舉例說明。

　　1998 年 12 月 10 日是 the Universal Declaration of Human Rights（世界人權宣言）在經過聯合國大會通過後的第 50 週年紀念日。美國總統柯林頓曾宣佈這一天為 Human Rights Day（人權日）。他在公告的前半段強調美國在國際社會致力維護與支持人權的行動上扮演著不可或缺的角色之後，以下述作結。

　　IN WITNESS WHEREOF, I have hereunto set my hand this tenth day of December, in the year of our Lord

nineteen hundred and ninety-eight, and of the Independ-ence of the United States of America the two hundred and twenty-third.（以此為證，吾人在此，於西元 1998 年 12 月 10 日，也是美利堅合眾國獨立第 223 年的今天，簽署了這份公告。）

In witness whereof (*or* thereof) 這些字一般使用於條約或證書上，很特別地，這份公告也使用了此一鄭重其事的字眼。不僅將西元年以字母拼出，還特別加註「美國年」。

日本在第二次世界大戰之前，也曾同時使用「昭和」和「皇紀」記年。「日本書記」中記載神武天皇即位之年為「皇紀元年」，比「西曆」還要早 660 年，所以「西元 2000 年」相當於「皇紀 2660 年」。《神社曆》的封面也同時記載「皇紀」和「西元」，但實際上，現今已經沒有人使用「皇紀」記年了。

不過，在回教國家裡，仍有使用「回曆」（西元 622 年為元年）的習慣，而猶太教徒也還在使用「猶太曆」（西元前 3761 年為元年）。

Part 3

中文寫作的小祕方

簡短、易懂的句子

我們寫文章的主要目的，在於要將自己想表達的訊息傳給讀者，所以讓讀者能立即且正確地理解訊息，實為寫作的最優先考量。

當然有時需視對象的不同而異，但書寫者也必須多加留意寫作的要領才對。若太自以為是，反而容易造成對方在理解方面上的困擾。因此書寫時，必須多方掌握訊息的內容、文章的結構、表達的方法到語彙的選擇等各個層面，另外也必須留意本書前半部提到的標點符號用法。關於這些寫作要點，全世界各國都相同，並無差異。

◆美國總統的一般政治聲明

當我們寫作時，首先必須留意要寫得「簡短、易懂」。但怎樣才算「短」，卻很難一概而論。讓我們先閱讀下列三段短文。每一段都是從美國的前三任總統 (Ronald Reagan, George Bush 及 Bill Clinton) 就職一年後，於 1 月在國會演說的 State of the Union messages （一般政治聲明）中所節錄下來。

(1)　A year ago I asked all of you to join me in accepting responsibility for the future of our country.—(20 words) [Clinton] （一年前，我曾要求各位和我一起共同承擔國家的未來。）

(2)　It is time to offer our hand to the emerging democracies

of Eastern Europe so that continent, for too long a continent divided, can see a future whole and free. — (30 words) [Bush] （現在正是我們向東歐的新興民主主義國家伸出援手的時刻，讓分裂多年的東歐能看見完全自由的未來。）

(3) That is why I can report to you tonight that in the near future the State of the Union and the economy will be better —much better—if we summon the strength to continue on the course we have charted.—(40 words) [Reagan] （因此，我得以在今晚向各位報告，只要我們鼓起勇氣繼續朝向我們規劃的路線前進，相信不久的將來，我國的狀況和經濟會好轉——並且更加地好。）

(4) When the earth shook and fires raged in California, when I saw the Mississippi deluge the farmlands of the Midwest in a 500-year flood, when the century's bitterest cold swept from North Dakota to Newport News, it seemed as though the world itself was coming apart at the seams.—(50 words) [Clinton] （當大地震和火災吞噬加州；當我親眼看見密西西比河 500 年來最大的洪水淹沒中西部的農場；當本世紀最冷冽的寒流從北達科他侵襲至紐波特紐斯，這個世界彷彿就要從接縫處裂開了。）

看完之後，有什麼感想？其實不管讀起來（或聽起來）都是 (1) 最容易理解吧。這不僅因為它的字數較少，還因為它是三

例中唯一表達了 I asked you to do something. 這一個中心理念的緣故。

比較起來，因為 (2) 放入了 so that continent ∼，而且又用 for too long a continent divided 來解釋 that continent，所以整體上要比 (1) 複雜許多。至於 (3) 中加入 if we summon the strength ∼ 表示條件的副詞子句後，主詞即劃分為二：the State of the Union and the economy，另外再加上副詞子句的主詞 we，所以會比 (1) 更難懂。

(4) 整段則有 50 個單字，這樣的長度真讓人無法一口氣唸完，其中 when 引導的副詞子句有三個，除此之外，還有許多不同的主題內容混雜在一起，所以要能「立即正確地了解」似乎困難了些。不過，卻還能以 it seemed as though ∼ 所引導的主要子句簡潔地表現出說話者的權威，並在冗長的句子後以此子句做為總結。

大多數人應該都會同意「一句話表達一個想法」的 (1) 是最容易了解的句子。然而，我們無法經常重複十多次同樣的句型來寫信、寫報導，甚至撰寫論文。畢竟句子的單字數、結構和遣詞用字也必須富於變化才對。不過，最重要的還是時時要記住「簡短、易懂」的寫作訣竅。

平均約為 20～30 words 的句子，可以說是最適當的長度，也是在非刻意的情況下唸起來最不吃力的長度。至於新聞媒體所報導的句子，平均大約 15～20 個字左右。

若是認為寫短句很容易，就是天大的誤解了。曾經寫過英文文章，或者將母語翻譯成英文的人，大概都經驗過不知不覺中會將句子寫得太長的情形。其實想要寫出簡短的佳句，必須要有充分掌握內容且判斷句子節奏感的能力。總之，要記住寫

作的重點在於「句子要儘量簡短、易懂」。

◆日本首相演講的譯文

先前介紹過美國總統的 State of the Union messages，接下來比較日本首相在國會發表的政策聲明 (policy speeches) 的英譯文。現今我們已可以從日本首相官邸的網頁 (http://www.kantei.go.jp/) 上看到日本首相重要演講的英譯文。

先談橋本首相在 1996 年 1 月 22 日所發表的演講，這次演講相當長，原文內容即佔了報紙一個版面的篇幅。其中在「創造一個人人嚮往長壽的美好社會」的小標題下，首相發表了如下演說：

在二十一世紀超高齡化的社會裡，由於中老年人口持續增加、年輕人口不斷減少，此時要如何維持、增進國家的活力，端看我們如何讓女性及老人更積極參與社會活動，以及如何因應在此之前完全靠家人照顧的老人及幼兒的看護問題，及其費用負擔方式，如何提供兒童們一個可取代家庭的環境等等，這些重要的課題都必須構思有系統性的完整解決方案。

此段落的英譯文如下：

In the superannuated society of the 21st century, with the middle-aged and older population growing larger and the younger population growing smaller, how well we are able to sustain and grow the nation's vitality will depend on how well we facilitate more active participation in society by women and older people, and this in turn is a question of what support society is able to

provide on caring for the elderly, child-care, and other issues that have traditionally been handled in the home, how we approach and devise the costing modalities, what kind of home-alternative environment we are able to create for children, and many other critical issues, and it is imperative that we create the systems needed to deal with these issues.

讀過一遍之後，不難想像譯者一定翻得很辛苦，極盡可能地將原文忠實地譯出，專業程度也令人佩服。儘管如此，考慮到原文是一個句子就翻譯成一個超過 120 個字的英文句子，也實在過於冗長，無法一口氣，不，連二口氣都讀不完。由於許多內容要點硬是被擠在一塊，所以也導致了這個句子的焦點模糊、主旨不明確。還好是翻譯的文章可以反覆閱讀，如果是美國總統在國會唸出這段譯文的話，多數的議員大概會歪著頭納悶地想「他在說什麼？」。所以至少應該將這段話劃分成兩個或三個句子，讓主題明確跳出，並且讓人一目了然。

◆美國總統 vs. 日本首相

下表是比較三位美國總統的 State of the Union messages 和日本三位首相「政策聲明」中英譯句子的字數統計表。( ) 內是佔句子總數的百分比 (%)。

句中的字數	～10	11～20	21～30	31～40	40～50	51～	句數
Reagan (1982)	43 (17.6)	93 (38.1)	59 (24.2)	33 (13.5)	10 (4.1)	60 (2.5)	共計 244 (100)
Bush (1990)	64 (28.6)	103 (46.0)	37 (16.5)	17 (7.6)	3 (1.3)	0 (0)	共計 224 (100)

Clinton (1994)	96 (24.7)	149 (38.3)	100 (25.7)	26 (6.7)	9 (2.3)	9 (2.3)	共計 389 (100)
細川護熙 (8/23/93)	2 (2.3)	14 (16.1)	15 (17.2)	19 (21.8)	15 (17.2)	22 (25.3)	共計 87 (100)
橋本龍太郎 (1/22/96)	5 (2.9)	30 (17.1)	28 (16.0)	37 (21.2)	34 (19.4)	41 (23.4)	共計175 (100)
小淵惠三 (8/7/98)	10 (7.2)	38 (27.5)	36 (26.1)	29 (21.0)	15 (10.9)	10 (7.2)	共計138 (100)

　　如先前所述，平均一個句子約有 20～30 words，且能夠不費力地一口氣讀完的長度才是最適當的句子。下表為從上表中計算出低於 20～30 words 的句子佔總數的百分比 (%)。

	（20 個字以內）	（30 個字以內）
雷根總統	55.7%	79.9%
布希總統	74.6	91.1
柯林頓總統	63.0	88.7
細川首相	18.4	35.6
橋本首相	20.0	36.0
小淵首相	34.7	60.8

　　雖然同樣都是美日領袖對議員所做的演說，但是由於日本首相的演說是譯文，所以實在無法單純就句子的長度做比較、討論。然而，在看過三位首相的演說稿原文之後，也就知道事實上有許多過長的句子，也許這就是如同大多數人所批評的，是日本官員所寫的文章之故。

　　相反地，三位美國總統的演說中，短句子居多，20 個字以內的句子就佔了近二分之一到三分之二。不過，雖說日本首相

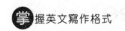

的英譯句子普遍過長，但在三位首相的政策聲明的譯文中，小淵首相演講的句子就顯得較短，這點倒也很引人注目。應該是譯者為了翻成淺顯易懂的文章，下了相當大的功夫。

◆報紙的社論

　　讓我們來看看性質和政治家的演說截然不同的報紙社論。由於新聞報導的種類多樣化，句子的平均長度也有相當大的差異，在此僅選定一般社論來討論。從代表英美的兩大報 *The Times* 和 *The Washington Post* 中，分別選出五天五篇主題相同的社論：有關在 1998 年 12 月 16 日到 20 日期間，世界的焦點都投射在英美兩國軍隊對伊拉克的空襲行動和美國眾議院決議通過彈劾柯林頓的發展這兩件事情。和前述分析政治家的演說一樣，依句子中字數的多寡加以分類後，得到以下的結果（句數為五篇社論的總計數）。（　）內為百分比 (%)。

句中的字數	～10	11～20	21～30	31～40	40～50	51～	句數
The Times	31	41	40	22	7	4	共計 145
	(21.4)	(28.3)	(27.6)	(15.2)	(4.8)	(2.7)	(100)
The Washington Post	14	42	31	13	3	1	共計 104
	(13.5)	(40.4)	(29.8)	(12.5)	(2.9)	(0.9)	(100)

　　同樣地，我們再分別以 20 個字以內和 30 個字以內的句子來分析所佔社論總句數的百分比：

	（20 個字以內）	（30 個字以內）
The Times	49.7%	77.3%
The Washington Post	53.9	83.7

　　就句子的長度來看，我們了解到性質差異極大的社論和總統演說兩者之間並沒有明顯的差別。談到社論，大部分的人多半會有句子長、用字遣詞艱澀的印象。但是，藉由上述分析，可以明白實際的情形和一般認知有相當大的差距。

　　總之，請牢記寫作目標必須首先注意：要以「簡潔」為最高原則。

② 如何寫得簡潔？

　　如先前所述，要想寫出一個簡短易懂的句子，最有效的方法是利用一個主詞和一個想法來表達。當然，這不是法條，不必約定俗成。而且，如果一篇文章到處充斥簡短的句子時，反而顯得單調無趣，甚至可能導致負面的效果。不過，雖說花點心思利用較複雜的句型使整體文章變得豐富、精彩是必要的，但是對於初學寫作的人來說，將 "One sentence, one idea." 當作撰寫句子的基本概念才是最重要的寫作入門原則。

　　如果想要寫得簡潔，首先必須留意下列會使句子加長的要點，以儘量避免。

◆留意關係詞的使用

　　關於加長句子的方法，首先可舉出兼具代名詞和連接詞功能的關係代名詞 (relative pronoun)，和兼具副詞和連接詞兩種功能的關係副詞 (relative adverb)。前者為 who, which, that, what 四種（另有 who 的所有格 whose，受格 whom），後者為 when, where, why, how 和以 -ever 結尾的 wherever, whenever, however

等複合關係副詞 (compound relative adverb)。這些關係詞因為可將兩個句子連接成一個句子，所以使用方便，但是相對地句子也會變長。

再就之前出現的英國 *The Times* 和美國 *The Washington Post* 的社論舉例說明。（關係詞以斜體字表示）

Iraq undertook last month to surrender vital documents *that* it had snatched from the inspectors *who* discovered them. — [*The Times*]（伊拉克曾經奪取軍事監察員所發現的重要文件，不過已於上個月開始交出。）

Mr. Clinton may find that those *who* live by opinion polls also perish by them.—[*The Times*]（柯林頓總統也許會發現，藉由民意調查而活躍的人也會毀於民意調查。）

A bombing campaign must be serious and sustained enough to gravely damage Saddam Hussein's weapons of mass destruction and the military forces upon *which* he depends for survival.—[*The Washington Post*]（空襲必須要能對海珊總統的大量毀滅性武器及其賴以為生的軍事力量造成嚴重且持續性的重大損害。）

要寫出稍微複雜的英文句子，就得借助關係詞。若使用得恰當，文章便能顯得紮實有力；但是，若過度使用，整個句子就會變得冗長難懂。

比較起來，*The Times* 和 *The Washington Post* 社論中的句子之所以顯得短，就是由於關係詞的使用頻率少的緣故。*The Times* 的五篇社論中，句子的總數為 145 句，關係代名詞用了十七次，而關係副詞只用了兩次，複合關係副詞則是零次。另一方面，*The Washington Post* 五篇社論的句子總數為 104 句，關

係代名詞雖然用了二十多次，但是並沒有出現任何關係副詞和複合關係副詞。

◆分詞構句也相同

讓句子變長的關鍵因素除了使用關係詞之外，還有就是使用分詞構句 (participial construction) 的緣故。在 *The Times* 和 *The Washington Post* 中各可看到一例。(分詞以斜體字表示)

This joint air campaign against Iraq is a watershed, *breaking* with the pattern of the past seven years in two important respects. —[*The Times*] (英美對伊拉克的聯合空襲行動是個轉換點，在兩項重要方面告別了過去七年以來的模式。)

Then, just about one year ago, the administration and its allies in Europe shrunk even their efforts at public diplomacy, *abandoning* their campaign to draw attention to China's human rights record.—[*WP*] (然而，大約在一年前，柯林頓政權和歐盟國家減少在國際外交政策上的努力，不再採行以往喚起人們關注中國人權政策的行動。)

常寫英文的人，一定有過在主要子句之後加上 saying that ～ 和 adding that ～ 這類分詞構句的經驗。

The president said that he would do everything possible to bail his deficit-ridden company out of its present crisis. (總裁表示將盡自己最大的努力以解救公司目前的負債危機。)

使用分詞構句時，可在一句話外再附加一個說明句：

——, adding that he would step down if his efforts to turn the situation around in two years failed. （——並表示，若他的努力未能在兩年之內使情況有所轉變的話，他願意下臺。）

——, expressing his hope that the business outlook would turn for the better next year. （——並表達希望明年的景氣會好轉。）

——, warning, however, that the union would have to accept a 10-percent wage cut or face an elimination of 100 jobs. （——並警告，若工會不願意接受刪減 10% 工資的話，將會解雇 100 個人。）

如上述，可以明白分詞構句使用起來既簡單又方便，且由於為同一個主詞，讀者唸起來也不會感到吃力。但是，仍須留意不要讓句子變得過長。若主要子句太長，則應避免使用分詞構句，而如下例另起一個句子較好。

He added that ～

He expressed his hope that ～

He warned, however, that ～

◆避免冗詞贅語

有時我們會在不了解或自以為是的情況下，使用過於冗長的字詞 (redundancy)。應該可以用一句話結束的句子，卻絮絮叨叨地說個沒完。為求句子簡潔，應該避免不必要的贅述，以免畫蛇添足。請參考以下可以寫得更簡潔的例子。

advance warning   → warning

after the conclusion of   → after

at this point in time	→ now
consensus of opinion	→ consensus
for the purpose of	→ for
if and when	→ if
in the course of	→ in (*or* during, while)
regardless of the fact that	→ although
unless and until	→ unless (*or* until)
whether or not	→ whether

3 S＋V＋O是寫出「道地英文」的起點

詢問學生英文的特性有哪些時，可以得到許多不同的答案。歸納總結後，可以如下所示：

主詞明確

單數、複數一目了然

主觀意識濃厚

重視邏輯、理性

果斷、清楚、明確

以動作為中心、較具動態性質

強烈的具體性

說到「道地英文」，相信有不少人還會馬上想到英文的片語 (phrase) 或慣用語的表達 (idiomatic expression) 方式。這些確實重要，但都不是最大的要點。如何擅用句法的結構以表達所要呈現的文章內容才是重點所在。

　　稍微學過英文的人都能將「她有兩個妹妹」的句子翻譯成 "She has two younger sisters."。表示狀態的「有」字變成英文的 "has"，這是運用到英文句法結構中最基本的句型：S + V + O（主詞 + 動詞 + 受詞）。

　　英文的五種基本句型整理如下：

S (= subject) 主詞

V (= verb) 動詞　　　　Vi (= intransitive verb) 不及物動詞

　　　　　　　　　　　Vt (= transitive verb) 及物動詞

C (= complement) 補語

O (= object) 受詞　　　O₁ (= direct object) 直接受詞

　　　　　　　　　　　O₂ (= indirect object) 間接受詞

句型 I (S + Vi)

Birds are chirping in the bush.

They have lived in Japan for two months.

句型 II (S + Vi + C)

He became a politician.

We agreed to meet once a year.

She went shopping.

句型 III (S + Vt + O)

They loved each other.

He is learning to speak Japanese.

I enjoyed reading your letter.

She said that she felt very lonely.

句型 IV (S + Vt + O₁ + O₂)

He gave me valuable suggestions.

I told him that he was right.

She didn't tell him what to do next.

句型 V (S + Vt + O + C)

I found him reliable.

He rejected my suggestion as unrealistic.

I heard the woman sobbing.

She couldn't make herself understood.

He kept me waiting for more than an hour.

前述英文的特色中，指出英文是「主觀意識濃厚」、「具動態性質」，除此之外，英文亦有將主詞（包含無生物）和周圍（包含無生物）之間的相互影響 (interaction) 當成句子中心的特性。主詞和周圍並非毫無關聯性，而是相互影響的對象，這點似乎就是英文的精髓所在。以英文為母語的人通常在遇到以上述句型撰寫的句子時，都會感到熟悉不突兀，讀來輕鬆不費力。像這樣的英文（或者接近這樣的英文）就是所謂的「道地英文」。

將電視播放的新聞翻成英文試試看。

「昨天晚上，在長野縣北部有相當強烈的地震，不過並沒有傷亡的報告。」

在生活中，我們經常可以聽到「有地震」、「有火災」、「有車子追撞事故」這類的消息。當我們要翻譯「有」字時，自然會想起「桌子上有一本書」的英文，即 "There is a book on the

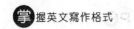

table."。若模仿此句將上述新聞的前半句譯成下例：

Last night, there was a fairly strong earthquake in northern Nagano Prefecture.

上句在文法上和拼字上都沒有錯誤，算是及格的英文。但是，總覺得尚有不佳之處。建議可以將表示時間的 last night 移到句尾較好。

There was a fairly strong earthquake in northern Nagano Prefecture last night.

這麼一來，句子就顯得沈穩。但是，仍然稍感不足，我們應該可以改得更好。

首先，there is 的構句缺乏震撼力。畢竟「地震」不像「桌上的書」一樣，只被當成一種「存在物」。雖說「相當強烈的地震」為無生物，但確實搖撼了「長野縣北部」的大地，令人們受到驚嚇。所以「相當強烈的地震」和「長野縣北部」可以成為動作主體（主詞）和受其影響的對象（受詞）的關係。如此一來，就和英文句法結構中基本句型的第 III 句型完全吻合，整句的震撼力也隨之加強。也就是說可以改寫成下列句子：

A fairly strong earthquake shook northern Nagano Prefecture last night.

另外，「相當強烈的地震」除了使用 shook 之外，也可以改用 jolted, rocked 或 hit, struck 來表達。

關於新聞後半句的處理方式，由於是短句，所以可以用逗點與前半句分開，寫成下列句子：

but no damage has been reported.

but there have been no reports of damage.

又例如日常生活中，我們經常使用「因～」、「由於～」的字眼。譬如「因一陣強風，吹起了數十片屋瓦」，以及「由於強勁的暴風雪，使得東京和北海道之間的航班失序」的句子。在聽到這些句子時，會反射性地想用 due to ～ 或者 because of ～ 來造句，結果產生了以下例句。

Scores of roof tiles were blown away due to a gusty wind.

Air service between Tokyo and Hokkaido was thrown into confusion because of a severe snowstorm.

雖然上述的構句也沒錯，但是事件起因的「陣風」和「暴風雪」應作為動作主體，也就是說，書寫時應將其視為主詞。此外，「若～」的條件用法亦可切換成主詞，如此才能將我們的母語自然而然地融入英文的句型型態中，也才能成為「道地英文」。順帶一提，以上兩個句子皆為被動語態 (the passive voice)。一般而言，被動語態比主動語態 (the active voice) 帶來的衝擊性較弱。若將「陣風」和「暴風雪」當作主詞，則產生下列句子：

A sudden gust of wind blew scores of tiles off the roof .

A severe snowstorm disrupted air service between Tokyo and Hokkaido.

又例如其他例句：

「走 10 分鐘就可以到達車站。」

Ten minutes' walk will bring you to the railroad station.

「若日幣持續升值，將使出口產業大受打擊。」

Further appreciation of the yen will deal a hard blow to the export industry.

A stronger yen will hit the export industry hard.

注：A stronger yen 表示「日幣若持續升值」的意思。因為還未發生，所以採用不定冠詞 a。「日幣升值」若已是事實或受大眾認定時，則改用 the strong yen。

另外，將母語中表示原因、條件的「因為～」、「由於～」、「若～」等字眼譯成英文時，不是反射性地採用英文的副詞片語或副詞子句就好，而應將其做為動作主體（主詞），將母語的主詞轉變成作用所及的客體（受詞），如此便可以很自然地變成第 III 句型。至於第 IV 和第 V 句型，可視為第 III 句型的延伸。

試著利用第 IV 和第 V 句型來處理以下的翻譯。

「董事長因工作過度勞累而賠上了健康。」

Overwork cost the president his health.（句型 IV）

「他因及時的道歉而免於受罰。」

A prompt apology spared him punishment. (IV)

A prompt apology saved him from punishment. (III)

「由於那本書非常有趣，所以我熬夜讀它。」

I found the book so interesting that I sat up all night reading it. (V)

「由於乾旱不斷，使得農作物的價格持續攀升。」

A long spell of dry weather has sent the prices of vegetables

soaring (*or* skyrocketing). (V)

當你將母語譯成英文或練習英文寫作時，何不試著努力多多套用第 III～V 句型，相信此份用心會有很大的收穫。等到熟能生巧，你會發現寫出來的句子很符合句型結構，同時也學到了書寫英文的「訣竅」。而寫出來的英文，在構句上也會接近「道地英文」，如此必定能讓以英文為母語的人在閱讀時，感到語句通順。

要成為英文寫作高手，就必須不斷地練習寫作技巧。而要寫出很棒的英文，就必須大量閱讀好的英文文章。當然，閱讀本身就是件很愉快的事；若能有毅力地為加強自身的書寫能力不斷地閱讀及練習書寫的話，相信一定會有更多收穫。

Coffee Break

3 個字為內容提要的 *NYT* 頭條新聞

The New York Times (*NYT*) 為美國最受高度信賴的報章媒體，一直是以 "All the News That's Fit to Print" 的座右銘成為聞名全球且最具公信力的報紙。

該報曾於 1956 年 3 月 1 日刊登了一則佔據一整個版面的頭條新聞，並以 3 個字做為內容提要：

WASHINGTON, Feb. 29—He said "yes."

在這個 dateline（註明地點及日期的日期欄）上面

的 byline（撰稿人署名處）印有 By James Reston（雷斯頓） 和 Special to The New York Times. 的字樣。

當天的標題就是所謂的 banner headlines，也就是橫跨整個版面兩端的特大標題。

EISENHOWER SAYS HE WILL SEEK A 2D TERM;
CONFIDENT OF HEALTH; BARS 'BARNSTORMING';
PRAISES NIXON BUT DOES NOT ENDORSE HIM

（艾森豪總統表明參選連任
對健康有信心；不會進行「巡迴演說」
欣賞尼克森但不支持他當副總統）

這是美國 1956 年總統大選前的報導。於該前一年 9 月心臟麻痺突然發作且已是 65 歲的 Dwight D. Eisenhower 總統是否會接受共和黨的提名競選連任一事，曾是當年美國人民最關心的話題。2 月 29 日晚間（當年為閏年），艾森豪總統透過廣播及電視演說發表了以下的談話：

"I have decided that if the Republican party chooses to renominate me, I shall accept."（本人決定，如果共和黨再度提名我參選，我會接受。）

於同年 11 月的選舉中，艾森豪總統以壓倒性的勝利擊敗了民主黨的候選人 Adlai E. Stevenson 而連任成功。

看得出記者對於報導的 lead（內容提要）很用心，

He said "yes." 也下得很正中標的。這種大膽且一針見血的三個字,很有 Reston 的個人風格。

Reston 在當時為美國最有名的記者,亦是 *NYT* 中評價最高的 The Washington Correspondent (華盛頓特派員)。他出生於英國蘇格蘭,後來移居美國,畢業於伊利諾州州立大學,曾當過伊利諾州前州長的高爾夫球球僮。後來,透過前州長的介紹,開始了當地報紙的新聞報導工作,這同時也是他記者生涯的開始。

之後,Reston 成為 AP 通訊社的體育記者,於 1939 年再轉往 *NYT*,到 1989 年 80 歲退休為止,有半個世紀之久一直是以 *NYT* 的著名記者身分聞名全美,曾取得無數的獨家大頭條,並分別於 1945 年及 1957 年二度榮獲代表記者最高榮譽的 Pulitzer Prize (普立茲獎)。他在辭去 *NYT* 的總編一職後,仍繼續為該報撰寫專欄。其以簡潔又有力的英文所寫出來的評論,不論是在美國或轉載海外,都受到相當多讀者的喜愛與好評。這名偉大的記者在 1995 年 12 月時與世長辭,享年 86 歲。

還有一個佔據 *NYT* 整個版面的頭條新聞之例,也是以三個字做為內容提要,是一篇於 1927 年所刊登的報導,早於 Reston 的 He said "yes." 的二十九年前刊出。內容提要如下:

PARIS, May 21—Lindbergh did it.

當年 Charles Lindbergh 駕駛著最喜愛的飛機 the Spirit of St. Louis,以 33 小時又 30 分的時間成功地從紐約飛

過 6,000 公里後抵達巴黎，成為世界第一位首次不著陸橫越大西洋的飛行者。報導此項歷史性創舉的報紙便成為振奮全世界的第一快報。

在 *NYT* 5 月 22 日的一個版面上，跳躍著下列的 banner headlines：

LINDBERGH DOES IT! TO PARIS IN 33 1/2 HOURS;
FLIES 1,000 MILES THROUGH SNOW AND SLEET;
CHEERING FRENCH CARRY HIM OFF FIELD

（林白做到了！33 小時半後抵達巴黎

飛越了 1,000 英里的雪與霰

瘋狂的巴黎市民在機場熱烈迎接）

④ 名詞、名詞片語的寫作練習

英文最大特色在於主詞明確，這點已於前面（「S＋V＋O 為寫出『道地英文』的起點」）敘述過。由於英文不是以名詞 (noun) 為主詞就是以名詞片語 (noun phrase) 為主詞，所以稱之為「以名詞為主」的語言亦不為過。正因為如此，當我們將母語（及其背後的想法）轉寫成英文之際，就應該必須儘量寫成標準的名詞、名詞片語形式。如此一來，寫出的英文才會簡潔且較為「道地」。

「因為他沒來，所以他的同學們都非常失望。」

Because he did not come, his classmates were disappointed.

Classmates were disappointed because he did not come.

從結構上來說，上述二句是由 because 起首的從屬子句 (subordinate clause) 和以 classmates 為首的主要子句 (principal clause) 所構成的複合句 (complex sentence)。英文的意思明確，文法上亦無錯誤。

如果加上一句「因此，整個班上的氣氛完全變了」時，應該拿什麼當主詞呢？當然是「整個班上的氣氛」。如此一來，短短的一句話在母語裡就有「同學們」和「整個班上的氣氛」兩個主詞。不過，在英文裡，會以一個用被動語態，另一個用不及物動詞的形式來表現。

將「因為他沒有出現」改成「他的未出現」這樣的名詞片語，並改成主詞形式看看：

The fact that he did not come 或

His failure to come

接著，即可完成 S＋V＋O（第 III 句型）。也就是：

His failure to come disappointed his classmates.

His failure to come let down his classmates.

或者用 S＋V＋C（第 II 句型）表達：

His failure to come was a big disappointment to his classmates.

His failure to show up came as a disappointment to his classmates.

當確定使用這類變成主詞的名詞片語後，後面句子的主詞也可以 This 來接續，甚至當母語中兩個較短句子的彼此關聯性高時，亦可整合成一句英文。例如：

His failure to come disappointed his classmates. This greatly changed the atmosphere (*or* mood) at the class reunion.

His failure to come disappointed his classmates, bringing a marked change in the mood at the class reunion.

如先前所述，表示原因、條件的「因此～」、「當～」的字眼出現在句首的機會很多，因此在翻譯成英文時，會誘導我們容易使用 because ～ 或 if ～ 之類的副詞子句，這時就要試著想辦法將其名詞化。

例如，「當我想到 ～」當然可以翻成 "When I think of ～," 這樣的英文，不過，我們也可以試著改用 think 的名詞 thought 來造句看看。

「當他想起在九州偏遠的鄉間從事農作的年邁母親時，心裡就感到難過。」

The thought of his aged mother doing farm work in a remote village in Kyushu made him sad.

The thought of his aged mother...filled him with sadness.

He was saddened by the thought of his mother....

如果是「光想到 ～ 就 ～」的翻譯，可以用 The mere thought of ～ 來強調。同樣的道理，將表「看到 ～」的 see 改成 sight 看看。

「這個男人一看到警察就逃。」

The man ran away at the sight of a policeman.

要表現比 sight 更印象深刻、震撼（包含諷刺）的句子時，可使用 spectacle。

Millions of TV viewers were shocked at the bizarre spectacle of several policemen beating and kicking a young man. （數百萬名電視觀眾在看到一名年輕人被多位警察又打又踢的不尋常畫面時，都深感震驚。）

「是否～」通常會翻成 whether ～ or not。如果想要表達得更簡潔，可以使用名詞形式。

「讓所有的小學生學習英文是否為明智之舉，我個人採懷疑的態度。」

I doubt the wisdom of making all primary school pupils learn English.

I question the wisdom of making English a compulsory subject in primary schools.

上述句子將 whether it is wise [or not] 以 wisdom 一個字表達。以下是將 whether it is proper [or not] 改以名詞形式寫成的句子。

「我們就廢除消費稅是否適當的問題進行討論。」

We debated the propriety of abolishing the consumption tax.

試著使用 whether ～ or not 的句型將下句翻譯成英文。

「政治改革的成功與否取決於首相是否能發揮領導能力。」

Whether political reform will succeed or not depends on whether the prime minister will be able to display leadership.

可以使用名詞形式的造句方式將上一句改成如下句般的簡潔。

Successful political reform depends on the prime minister's ability to display leadership.

若是會話或非正式的 (informal) 英文，不一定全都必須改成本單元中所強調的以名詞為主的構句方式。而且，也不能否認這樣的構句有時會給人艱澀難懂的印象。儘管我們無法完全脫離用自己的母語表達的習慣以及自身的思考模式，但為了寫出「道地英文」，我們必須具備彈性的應變能力，以便可以迅速將心中想表達的意念轉換成文法結構正確、主題清晰明確而不致艱澀難懂的英文句子。

5 不可數名詞的數詞用法

說到不可數名詞 (uncountable noun)，便會想到如 beer, chalk, water 等的「物質名詞」(material noun) 和 beauty, education, silence 等的「抽象名詞」(abstract noun)。這些名詞無法用一個、兩個等實際的數量來計算，也就是說無法像可數名詞一樣加 -s。

◆兼具可數與不可數性質的名詞

　　上述所做的說明只是個大概的原則。實際上，名詞當中有不少單字同時具有可數名詞和不可數名詞的性質。

(1)　Beer is an alcoholic drink made from malt and flavored with hops. （啤酒是一種以麥芽為原料，並用啤酒花調味的含酒精飲料。）

上例的 beer 為物質名詞，可以用 a glass of beer, two pints of beer 的方式來計算。另一方面，beer 也是可數名詞。

(2)　He ordered two beers. （他點了兩杯啤酒。）

此例的 two beers 為 two glasses of beer 的意思，是可數名詞。同樣地，如 two teas (= two cups of tea), three coffees (= three cups of coffee) 也是以相同用法當作可數名詞。另外，cheese 的複數形為 cheeses。

(3)　Blood is thicker than water. （血濃於水。）
　　　Will you give me a glass of water?
　　　He asked for some water.

(4)　Most countries claim 12-mile territorial waters.
　　（大多數國家都主張 12 海里的領海權。）
　　　coastal [international] waters （沿岸 [國際] 海域）
　　　Elderly people used to come to this town to take the waters. （老年人以往為了泡溫泉而來到這個城鎮。）

例句 (3) 的 water 為物質名詞，而例句 (4) 的 waters 在形式上則被當作普通名詞。

　　一般被認為是抽象名詞的 education （教育）及 knowledge （知識），當變成如下列有具體性的性質時，用法同可數名詞。

(5)　They worked hard to give their children a good education. （為了提供小孩良好的教育，他們辛苦地工作。）

　　　He has a college education. （他受大學教育。）

　　　She had a Harvard education. （她曾就讀哈佛大學。）

(6)　He has a remarkable knowledge of Japanese manners and customs. （他非常熟知日本的風俗習慣。）

　　　She has only a limited knowledge of China. （她對中國的了解有限。）

例句 (5) 和 (6) 中，education, knowledge 的前面先接形容詞或者具限定之意的單字時，成為可數名詞，可用不定冠詞來修飾。不過，照理說，一般名詞若為可數名詞時，其複數形應該加上 -s，但請留意兩者都沒有加 -s。

(7)　Speech is silver, silence is golden. （雄辯是銀，沈默是金。）

　　　The children watched the movie in utter silence. （孩子們靜靜地看著電影。）

(8)　Suddenly a brief silence swept through the room. （突然間，一陣沈默劃過整個屋裡。）

　　　Their conversation was punctuated by awkward silences. （他們的對話屢次被令人尷尬的沈默打斷。）

例句 (8) 的 a silence 即為 a period of silence。因此，silences 也可改成 periods of silence。

如同上述幾例，有不少原本為抽象名詞，但之後常被當作普通名詞的例子，茲列舉其他單字如下：

[抽象名詞]	[普通名詞]
atrocity（殘酷）	an atrocity/atrocities（殘暴行為）
authority（權威）	[the] authorities（當局）
beauty（美麗）	a beauty/beauties（美人；優點）
cruelty（殘酷）	a cruelty/cruelties（殘酷行為）
damage（破壞；損害）	damages（損害賠償）
future（未來）	futures（期貨）
honor（名譽）	honors（優異成績；勳章）
hostility（敵意）	hostilities（戰爭；戰鬥行為）
strength（力量）	a strength/strengths（強度）
utility（效用）	utilities（公營事業）
youth（年輕）	a youth/youths（年輕人）
weakness（軟弱）	a weakness/weaknesses（弱點）

要敘述不可數名詞的數量時，可以利用以下的詞語表示大概的數量及程度。

We have {
much/a lot of/lots of/
a great deal of/some/
a little/a bit of/bits of/no
}

information on the new president.

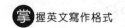

We hardly have any information on the new president.

若要一個個指出且具體予以數量化時，則必須要用 a piece of ～, two pieces of ～, three pieces of ～ 等表達。piece 為不可數名詞數量化後的單位名詞 (unit noun)。

將「他給我忠告」翻成英文時，可以發現有下列幾種說法：

(a) He gave me advice.

(b) He gave me some advice.

(c) He gave me sound advice.

(d) He gave me a piece of advice.

(e) He gave me a sound piece of advice.

表現具體的印象或數量時，須用 (d)、(e) 的形式。若 (e) 改成：

(f) He gave me a piece of sound advice.

則為東方式的說法。在英文的語法上，由於 a piece of 和接下來的名詞關係密切，所以將原本 (c) 的 sound advice 分開，而用 sound 來修飾整個 a piece of advice。以下二例的語法亦同。

(g) They gave us *a fascinating piece of information* on the new president.（他們提供我一些新任總裁的趣聞。）

(h) He produced *an extremely effective piece of evidence* against the defendant.（他提出一個對被告非常不利的有力證據。）

在此再舉出幾個代表性的名詞。這些名詞和 advice 一樣，是不可數名詞，在數詞用法上，也採用 a piece of/pieces of 或類

似的單位名詞表示。

advice	（忠告）	(a piece of ～, a word of ～)
baggage(*or* luggage)	（行李）	(a piece of ～)
clothing	（衣服）	(an article of ～, an item of ～, a piece of ～)
equipment	（設備）	(a piece of ～)
evidence	（證據）	(a piece of ～)
furniture	（家具）	(a piece of ～, a stick of ～)
homework	（家庭作業）	(a piece of ～)
information	（資訊）	(a piece of ～, an item of ～)
legislation	（法律）	(a piece of ～)
mail	（郵件）	(a piece of ～)
news	（新聞）	(a piece of ～, an item of ～)
work	（工作）	(a piece of ～)
writing	（著作）	(a piece of ～)

注 1：一般來說，特別是在會話上，會經常使用 a bit 代替 a piece。

注 2：e-mail（電子郵件）被當作普通名詞，寫成 an e-mail 或 e-mails。

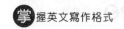

◆主要的單位名詞

除了介紹 piece, bit 以外，在此再列舉一些主要的單位名詞，同時於其後加上幾個可以接續的不可數名詞或可數名詞為例。

a bar of ～/ bars of ～（長方形或堅硬的條狀物）：chocolate, gold, soap, etc.

beam （光線）：light, moonlight/delight, hope, etc.

blade （薄又平坦的葉狀物）：grass, rice, wheat, etc.

block （堅硬且大塊的東西）：ice, stone, wood/seats, votes, etc.

chunk （大塊、厚片的東西）：cake, coal, bread, cheese, meat, stone/capital, money, etc.

clod （土塊）：earth, clay, turf, etc.

coil （捲曲的東西）：hair, rope, etc.

crumb （麵包、糕餅等的碎屑）：bread, cake, comfort/ information, knowledge, etc.

dash （微量的液體、攪和物）：gin, lemon, juice, oil, soda, whiskey, etc.

dose（一次的藥量）：medicine, antibiotics, aspirin, radiation/ bad news, flattery, love, etc.

drop （微量的液體）：rain, water, oil, wine/compassion, kindness, etc.

flake（薄的碎片）：snow, stone, plaster, etc.

grain（穀類的顆粒、微量）：corn, rice, salt, sand/intelligence, truth, etc.

item（商品的一個單項）：clothing, information, mail, news, etc.

length（丈量物體的長度）：cloth, pipe, rope, string, tubing, wire, etc.

loaf/loaves（麵包、蛋糕的切塊）：bread

lump（手可以拾起的塊狀物）：clay, coal, earth, sugar/ money, greed, etc.

pane（窗玻璃片）：glass

pinch/pinches（一小撮的量）：incense, cinnamon, salt, snuff/ indignation, malice, etc.

puff（少量的煙、氣體）：air, dust, smoke, steam, wind, etc.

roll（捲狀物）：bread, carpet, film, hair, wallpaper, etc.

scrap（碎片）：food, meat, paper/conversation, evidence, gossip, information, news, truth, etc.

sheaf（束，捆）：barley, corn, wheat/autographs, documents, letters, etc.

sheet（板子或薄片）：ice, glass, paper, plastic, rain, flame, etc.

shot（小玻璃杯一杯的量；藥物的一劑）：gin, whiskey, cocain, morphine, etc.

shred（長條物的碎片）：cloth, clothing, paper/doubt, evidence, etc.

slab（較寬的厚板）：bread, cake, metal, stone, wood, etc.

slice（薄切片）：bread, cake, ham, meat, toast/life, profits, etc.

sliver（又小又薄的裂片）：cake, cheese, glass, etc.

speck（細片；小斑點）：blood, dirt, dust, grit/good, truth, light, etc.

squeeze（搾取的少量汁液）：lemon juice, lime, oil, etc.

stick（細長形的棒狀物）：candy, celery, chalk, dynamite, furniture, etc.

strand（多股絞合的繩狀物）：cotton, hair, wire, wool, yarn, pearls, etc.

wad（小的團狀物）：butter, cotton, gum/bills, dough（現款）, etc.

6 Letter 和 Message 的差別─可接同位語的名詞

(1)✕ I received a letter from him that he would visit Japan next year.

(2) I received a message from him that he would visit Japan next year.

為何 (1) 會打✕（表示錯誤的符號）呢？為什麼 (2) 才是正確的句子？letter 和 message 到底有何差別？

為了慎重起見，首先查閱手邊的辭典 (*Longman Dictionary of Contemporary English*) 以茲確認。

letter: a written or printed message sent usu. in an envelope

message: a spoken or written piece of information passed from one person to another.... [+ *that*] Did you get the message that your boss has canceled the meeting?

也就是說，letter 為「用手寫或印刷的訊息，通常會放入信封來傳送」的東西。而 message 則定義為「透過人和人口語的傳達或者書寫的一項資訊」，並舉一個例句說明其後可接 that 子句當同位語。letter 則沒有註明是否可以接表同位語的子句，而其原意為「手寫或印刷的訊息」，指的是書寫訊息的紙張，和重點在「資訊」的 message 的性質不同。另外，telegram 也和 letter 的接續方式相同。

接著，將 (1) 改成以下正確的英文：

I received a letter from him saying that he would visit Japan next year.

I received a letter from him in which he said that he would visit Japan next year.

現在的辭典在編排上已有很大的進步，皆強調「方便使用者」(user-friendly)，但是還未曾見過將所有可以接同位語的名詞全部條列出來的辭典。

寫英文時，有時不免會對該名詞是否可接同位語的問題感到困擾。先假設可以接後再查閱辭典，如果辭典上有註明 [+ that]，就會感到很高興。相反地，如果沒有明示可以 [+ that]，就會覺得很不妥。不過，即使再厚的辭典也無法像上述一樣回

答得一清二楚。若是光靠直覺判斷，畢竟也會不放心。難道可接同位語的名詞和不可接同位語的名詞之間沒有規則可循嗎？謹在此藉由以前累積的經驗，試著整理如下。

可接同位語的名詞，大致上可分為以下三大類。

（1）　如 fact（事實），legend（傳說），news（新聞）等單純名詞，可說是一聽到該字就能對其內容充分掌握。下列名詞也可以歸納為這一類：

adage（箴言），consensus（一致），doctrine（教義），faith（信念），fiction（虛構），gospel（信條），hunch（預感），hypothesis（假設），idea（想法），maxim（格言），moral（道德上的教訓），myth（神話），opinion（意見），proverb（諺語），tip（暗示）等。

（2）　本身另有形容詞變化的名詞。可再區分為以下兩類：
(a) 本身另外具有單純形容詞的名詞。

confidence　（信　　心）　（← confident)
likelihood　（可　能　性）　（← likely)
optimism　　（樂觀主義）　（← optimistic)
pessimism　　（悲觀主義）　（← pessimistic)
possibility　（可　能　性）　（← possible) 等。

另外如 happiness, sadness 本身也有 happy, sad 的形容詞，但這兩個名詞和上面所列的名詞不同，不接 that 子句，通常會如下列例句採取 a feeling of ～, a sense of ～ 的形式表達。

He expressed a sense (*or* feeling) of happiness that his daughter gave birth to a boy. （他為女兒生了個男孩感到高興。）

(b) 此類名詞另外有由動詞轉化的形容詞，而其形容詞原本為動詞變化後的過去分詞。

conviction （確信）(← convinced)

delight （喜悅）(← delighted)

disappointment （失望）(← disappointed)

satisfaction （滿意）(← satisfied)

surprise （驚奇）(← surprised) 等。

（3） 由動詞衍生而來的名詞。

The people reacted angrily to the government's announcement that the consumption tax would be increased from 3 percent to 5 percent. （民眾對政府宣佈要將消費稅由 3% 提高至 5% 表示不滿。）

上述句子的結構當然是以 the government announced that ～ 為基礎。在接同位語的名詞當中，此類型的單字最多。以 -ment, -sion, -tion 為結尾的名詞即屬於此類。

acknowledgement （承認）, admission （告白）, agreement （同意）, commitment （公約）, confession （坦白）, explanation （說明）, profession （聲明）, speculation （推測）, suggestion （建議）等。

◆不可接 that 子句當同位語的主要名詞

有很多名詞看似可以接 that 子句當同位語，但實際上卻無法接續。在此舉出一些一般人常會弄錯的幾個主要名詞。請留意以下幾個不能接 that 子句的名詞，而箭頭後另外列出可取代 that 的關係詞。

case （情形）　There have been a number of cases in which boys under 15 have been drafted into guerrilla forces. (有很多 15 歲以下的男孩被徵召當游擊隊員的情況。) → in which 也可用 where 取代。

注：case 代表法庭上的「主張、申辯」的意思時，可接當同位語的 that 子句。

circumstances （情況）→ in which, where

condition 　　　（狀態）→ in which, where

注：condition 表示「條件」的意思時，可接當同位語的 that 子句。

situation （情況）→ in which, where

◆可接 that 子句當同位語的名詞

接下來列舉可接 that 子句當同位語的名詞，不過並非全部，僅限於常見的單字為主。

accusation （指責；控告）, acknowledgment （承認）, adage （諺語）, admission （承認）, admonition （忠告）, advantage （優勢）, advice （忠告）, affidavit （宣誓書）, affirmation

（確認）, agreement（同意）, alarm（驚慌）, allegation（主張）, analysis（分析）, announcement（發表）, anxiety（憂慮）, appeal（上訴）, appearance（外觀）, apology（道歉）, apprehension（憂心）, argument（爭論）, assertion（主張）, assumption（假定）, assurance（保證）, attitude（態度）, awareness（意識；體認）

bargain（協議）, belief（信念）, bet（賭注）, bias（偏見）, bitterness（悲痛）, bulletin（新聞快報）

care（憂慮）, case（主張）, caution（警告）, chance（可能性）, charge（指責）, claim（要求）, clamor（叫喊）, cliché（陳腔濫調）, clue（線索）, coincidence（巧合）, commitment（委託）, complaint（抱怨）, concern（擔心）, conclusion（結論）, condition（條件）, confession（承認）, confidence（信賴）, confirmation（確認）, consensus（一致）, contention（主張）, contract（契約）, conviction（確信）, corollary（必然的結果）, criticism（批評）, cry（哀求）

danger（危險）, decision（決定）, declaration（宣言）, delight（喜悅）, delusion（錯覺）, demand（要求）, demonstration（論證）, denunciation（斥責）, desire（渴望）, determination（決心）, dictum（格言）, difference（差異）, disadvantage（不利）, disappointment（失望）, disclosure（揭發）, discovery（發現）, displeasure（不滿）, dispute（爭論）, distinction（特質）, doctrine（教義）, dogma（教義）, doubt（懷疑）, dread（懼怕）, dream（夢）

effect（要旨）, entreaty（懇求）, estimate（估計）, [in the] event（～情況）, evidence（證據）, exception（例外）, exclamation（喊叫）, excuse（辯解）, expectation（期待）, explanation（說明）, extent（程度）

fact（事實）, factor（要素）, faith（信念）, fancy（幻想）, fear（害怕，恐懼）, feel（感覺）, feeling（感覺）, fiction（虛構）, finding（發現；判決）, foreboding（預感）, forecast（預報）, forewarning（預先警告）, formula（準則）, formulation（公式化）, front（外表）

generalization（概括）, gospel（信條）, ground（根據）, guarantee（保證）, guess（猜測）

hint（暗示）, honor（榮譽）, hope（希望）, hunch（預感）, hypothesis（假設）

idea（想法）, illusion（幻想）, image（訊息）, impeachment（指責）, implication（暗示）, importance（重要性）, impression（印象）, incantation（咒文）, indication（徵兆；證據）, indignation（憤慨）, inference（推論）, information（資訊）, injunction（命令）, inkling（暗示）, insight（洞察）, insinuation（奉承諂媚）, insistence（主張）, instinct（本能）, instruction（指示）, intelligence（情報）, interpretation（解釋）, intimation（暗示）, irony（出乎意料的結果）

justification（辯護）

knowledge（知識）

law（法律）, legend（傳說）, lesson（教訓）, likelihood（可

能性）, line（方針）, locution（語言風格）

maxim（格言）, meaning（意思）, merit（長處）, message（訊息）, mind（意見）, misconception（誤解）, misfortune（不幸）, mistake（錯誤）, moral（教訓）, morality（教訓）, murmur（低語聲）, myth（神話）

nature（性質）, news（新聞）, note（筆記）, notice（通知）, notification（通告）, notion（想法）

oath（誓言）, observation（意見）, odds（成功機率）, omen（預兆）, opinion（意見）, optimism（樂觀主義）, order（命令）, orthodoxy（正統說法）, outcry（強烈的抗議）, outlook（觀點）

paradox（自相矛盾的議論）, peculiarity（奇特）, perception（認識）, persuasion（說服）, phenomenon（現象）, philosophy（哲學）, plea（藉口）, pleading（辯護）, pledge（保證）, point（要點）, policy（政策）, position（立場）, possibility（可能性）, postulate（基本條件）, prayer（祈禱）, precept（訓誡）, prediction（預言）, preference（偏愛）, prejudice（偏見）, premise（前提）, premonition（預感）, presentiment（預感）, presumption（推測）, presupposition（假定）, pretense（藉口）, pride（自負）, principle（原則）, privilege（特權）, probability（或然性）, proclamation（宣佈）, profession（聲明）, projection（預測）, promise（承諾）, pronouncement（宣言）, proof（證據）, property（財產）, prophecy（預言）, proposal（提案）, proposition（提議）, prospect（前

途）, protestation（斷言）, proverb（諺語）, provision（規
定）, proviso（附帶條件）

question（疑問）

reality（現實）, realization（領悟）, reason（理由）, reasoning
（推理）, reassurance（再保證）, recognition（認識）,
recollection（回憶）, recommendation（勸告）, reflection（感
想）, refrain（疊句）, regret（遺憾）, relief（解脫的心
情）, remark（評論）, reminder（令人想起的東西）, reply
（回答）, report（報告）, request（要求）, requirement（要
求）, resentment（憤慨）, resolution（決議）, resolve（決
心）, restriction（限制）, result（結果）, revelation（暴
露）, riposte（機敏地反駁）, risk（危險）, rule（規定）, ruling
（裁定）, rumor（謠言）

saying（格言）, secret（祕密）, sensation（感覺）, sense（意
義）, sentiment（心情）, shock（衝擊）, shout（喊叫）, shouting
（喊叫）, sign（徵兆）, signal（信號）, skepticism（懷疑
論）, specification（詳述）, speculation（推測）, stance（立
場）, stand（態度）, statement（陳述）, stipulation（規
定）, story（故事）, suggestion（暗示；建議）, supposition
（假定）, surmise（推測）, surprise（驚喜）, suspicion（嫌
疑）

talk（談話；流言蜚語）, tenet（教義）, terms（條件）, terror
（恐懼）, testimony（證詞）, theme（主題）, theorem（原
理）, theory（理論）, thesis（命題）, thinking（思考）, thought

（想法）, threat （威脅）, tidings （祕密消息）, tip （情報）, tradition （傳說）, truism （明顯的事實）, truth （真實）

ultimatum（最後通牒）, unanimity（一致同意）, understanding （了解）, urgency （緊急）

verdict （判決）, version （說明）, view （觀點）, vindication （辯護）, voice （聲音）, vow （誓言）

warning （警告）, whisper （悄悄話）, willingness （自願）, wisecrack （俏皮話）, wish （願望）, word （消息；傳言）, worry （擔心）

7 可接補語的形容詞

有關哪些名詞可接 that 子句作同位語，已於前項單元「Letter 和 Message 的差別」中做過說明，本單元中要討論形容詞和 that 子句的關係。和名詞一樣，辭典對於哪些形容詞可接 that 子句和哪些不可以接的敘述並不多，此點亦為英文寫作和英語會話中很重要的一項課題。

「形容詞和 that 子句」是文法用語，列舉容易了解的英文例句如下：

(1) I'm *glad that* you could come to see me. （我很高興你能來看我。）

(2) He was *positive that* his father had told the truth. （他確信他的父親所言屬實。）

(3) She was *surprised that* her hometown had undergone

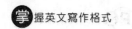

great changes.（她對故鄉的巨大改變感到吃驚。）

(4) He is *concerned that* the recession will get even worse.（他擔心經濟蕭條的情況會持續惡化。）

以斜體字表示的形容詞，分別表達了喜悅、確信、驚訝和擔心等意思，並以 that 子句作補充說明。這種構句方式經常使用於文章和會話中，然而無論在會話或文章中都常省略 that。

從上面的例句中，我們可將用於此種構句的形容詞分為兩大類。

例句 (1)、(2) 中的形容詞為所謂的單純形容詞，不過兩者的性質不同。

例句 (1) 若採「形容詞 + to 不定詞」的構句，即改成 I'm glad to know that you could come to see me. 時也能傳達相同的意思。同樣地，也適用於 happy, sad, sorry 等字。

I'm *happy* that you passed the test. (= I'm happy to know that you passed the test.)（我很高興你通過了考試。）

I'm *sorry* that your mother was injured in a car accident. (= I'm sorry to hear that your mother was injured in a car accident.)（聽到你母親車禍受傷的消息，我很難過。）

例句 (2) 無法置換成「形容詞 + to 不定詞」的構句。其他如 adamant, emphatic, insistent, optimistic, pessimistic, thankful 等字亦同。

She is *adamant* that she did the right thing.（她堅持自己所做的事是對的。）

He was *optimistic* that his proposal would be approved unanimously. （他樂觀地認為他的提案會獲得全場一致的同意。）

　　另外一種形容詞，是指本身原為動詞的過去分詞，後因動詞的意義轉弱而變成形容詞。

　　例句 (3) 和 (1) 一樣，可以用「形容詞 + to 不定詞」這種構句傳達相同的意思，即 She was surprised to see (*or* find) that her hometown had undergone great changes. 。或者像 She was surprised at the great changes that had taken place in her hometown. 使用介系詞的構句表達相同的意思。這種形容詞還有許多其他的構句方式。

I'm *relieved* that her mother is out of danger. （在得知她的母親脫離險境時，我鬆了一口氣。）(= I'm relieved to hear that her mother is out of danger./I'm relieved at the news that her mother is out of danger.)

　　例句 (4) 的 concerned 不能用「形容詞 + to 不定詞」替代。下面例句也相同。

He is *worried* that his deficit-ridden company will shed more jobs. （他擔心負債累累的公司還會繼續裁員。）

　　須留意不同的形容詞其後所接的 that 子句用法。anxious 就是其中一個例子。

He is *anxious* that he should get first place. （他渴望得到第一

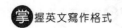

名。）(= He is anxious to get first place. = He is anxious for first place.)

He is *anxious* that we will bail him out of bankruptcy.（他巴望著我們救他免於破產。）(= He is anxious for us to bail him out of bankruptcy.)

接下來列舉一些可接 that 子句的主要形容詞。

（1）　單純形容詞（省略 be 動詞，括弧內為意思相似的同義字）

adamant （強烈主張的 = emphatic, insistent）

afraid （I'm *afraid* that the economy will remain stagnant for the rest of the year. 我擔心今年年底以前的經濟情況仍會持續蕭條。）

angry （He was *angry* that she did not come to his aid. 他生氣她沒有來幫忙。）

anxious （渴望的 = eager）

apprehensive （憂慮的 = worried）

aware （意識到的 = conscious）

careful （仔細的）

certain （確信的 = positive, sure）

comfortable （舒適的 = satisfied）

confident （確信的 = certain, sure）

conscious （意識到的 = aware）

eager （渴望的 = anxious）

emphatic（強烈主張的 = adamant, insistent）

fearful（害怕的 = afraid）

fortunate（幸運的 = lucky）

furious（狂怒的 = very angry）

glad（高興的 = happy, pleased）

grateful（感謝的 = thankful）

hopeful（期待的）

insistent（堅決的 = adamant, emphatic）

lucky（幸運的 = fortunate）

mindful（記住的 = aware）

optimistic（樂觀的）

pessimistic（悲觀的）

positive（確信的 = certain, sure）

proud（得意的）

resentful（忿恨的 = angry）

sad（悲傷的 = grieved）

sorry（遺憾的 = sad）

sure（確信的 = certain, positive）

thankful（感激的 = grateful）

unaware（未察覺到的）

unhappy（不快樂的）

（2） 由過去分詞轉換而成的形容詞（省略 be 動詞，括弧內為
同義字）

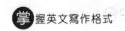

aggrieved（悲傷的 = sad）(She was/felt *aggrieved* that he had not written to her for more than a year.)（她感到悲傷，因為他已經一年多沒寫信給她了。）

agreed（意見一致的 [主詞為複數]）

amazed（吃驚的 = surprised）

amused（愉快的 = delighted）

annoyed（氣惱的 = angry, irritated）

appalled（驚駭的 = shocked）

assured（確信的 = certain）

astonished（驚訝的 = very surprised）

astounded（驚訝的 = astonished）

bewildered（困惑的 = puzzled）

concerned（擔心的 = worried）

confused（困惑的 = bewildered）

convinced（確信的 = certain, positive, sure）

delighted（高興的 = very glad）

determined（下定決心的）

disappointed（失望的 = frustrated）

discouraged（洩氣的 = frustrated）

disgusted（嫌惡的 = displeased）

elated（興高采烈的 = extremely happy, excited）

encouraged（受到鼓舞的 = heartened）

enraged（忿怒的 = very angry）

excited（興奮的 = thrilled）

flabbergasted（目瞪口呆的 = bewildered, confused）

flattered（奉承的 = pleased and proud）

frightened（受驚嚇的 = scared）

frustrated（洩氣的 = disappointed, discouraged）

gratified（滿意的 = satisfied）

grieved（傷心的 = very sad）

heartened（受到振奮的 = encouraged）

heartbroken（悲傷的 = very sad）

honored（感到榮譽的 = proud and happy）

horrified（驚懼的 = shocked）

impressed（印象深刻的）

irritated（惱怒的 = angry, annoyed）

irked（煩躁的 = annoyed, irritated）

offended（生氣的 = angry）

outraged（憤慨的 = very angry）

overjoyed（極度高興的 = very pleased）

pleased（高興的 = glad, happy）

persuaded（確信的 = convinced）

perturbed（感到不安的 = worried）

puzzled（困惑的 = bewildered）

reassured（使放心的）

relieved（寬慰的）

satisfied（滿足的 = content）

scared（令人恐懼的 = frightened）

shocked（震驚的 = surprised, upset）

slighted（受忽視的）

stunned（震驚的 = very surprised, shocked）

surprised（出人意外的 = astonished）

terrified（害怕的 = frightened, scared）

thrilled（激動的 = excited）

tickled/tickled pink（非常樂意的 = very pleased）

upset（苦惱的 = worried）

vexed（生氣的 = angry）

worried（擔心的 = concerned, upset）

8 「雙字動詞」的功能

　　「雙字動詞」(two-word verb) 對寫出簡單且道地的英文有非常大的幫助。也可以稱之為 verb-adverb combination（動副詞），phrasal verb（動詞片語）或 verb-particle combination（動質詞）。為了方便起見，一般包含動詞 + 副詞 + 介系詞（例如：put up with [忍耐]）的詞語，皆可稱為「雙字動詞」。請看下列例句：

(1)　(a) Both countries are <u>increasing</u> their armed forces. （兩國都在增強軍事力量。）

　　　(b) Both countries are *building up* their armed forces.

(2)　(a) He <u>withdrew</u> from the agreement at the last minute.
　　　　（他在最後關頭退出協議。）

　　　(b) He *pulled out* of (*or* from) the agreement at the last minute.

(3)　(a) The two countries <u>severed</u> their diplomatic relations.
　　　　（兩國斷絕外交關係。）

　　　(b) The two countries *broke off* their diplomatic relations.

(4)　(a) The scandal <u>disappointed</u> many of his supporters.（醜聞令許多支持他的人感到失望。）

　　　(b) The scandal *let down* many of his supporters.

(5)　(a) The security force <u>suppressed</u> the dissident groups.
　　　　（安全部隊鎮壓異議團體。）

　　　(b) The security force *cracked down on* the dissident groups.

　　以上所有例句的 (b) 中，以斜體字表示的詞語均為雙字動詞。此處出現的動詞 build, pull, break, let, crack 等都是單音節字 (monosyllable)，其字源均為古英語 (Old English)，也就是盎格魯撒克遜語 (Anglo-Saxon) 的簡單單字。這些字在結合了 up, down, off, out 等副詞之後，產生出淺顯易懂且活潑生動的語感，比起劃底線的多音節字 (polysyllable) 的發音更容易且更口語，再加上所接的副詞本身含有動作的「方向性」或「完成」之意，所以更能呈現出鮮明且具體的意象。

握英文寫作格式

有相當多雙字動詞的字源來自於 Anglo-Saxon。像拉丁語 (Latin) 只有 balance, branch, catch, measure, pass 等，數量並不多，而希臘語 (Greek) 中，即使包括片語 (phrase) 也都還數得出來有幾個。另外，動詞多半為單音節字，若是雙音節字 (bisyllabic)，則其重音會落在第一音節上。

可形成雙字動詞的主要副詞如下：

about, across, around, aside, away, back, by, down, forth, in, off, on, out, over, through, up

以上所列舉的副詞中，如 across, aside, forth 並不像 countdown, payoff, turnover 一樣有名詞用法 (nominalization)。

動詞在藉由和這些副詞相結合後，可將原本的不及物動詞變成及物動詞，反之，亦能將及物動詞變成不及物動詞。

·不及物動詞 → 及物動詞的例子：

He *laughed away* the rumored attempt on his life.（他對自己的生命受到威脅的謠言一笑置之。）

Go to bed early and *sleep off* your tiredness.（儘早就寢以消除疲勞。）

Look up the word in the dictionary.（用辭典查這個單字。）

·及物動詞 → 不及物動詞的例子：

Rebel resistance is reported to be *breaking down*.（根據報導，反抗軍的抵抗行動已經節節敗退。）

He *checked in* shortly after noon.（他一過中午就馬上登記住

168

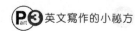

宿。)

Food supplies to the quake victims are *giving out*. (供應給地震災民的糧食即將耗盡。)

使用雙字動詞寫作時,應留意與動詞 + 介系詞的不同:

(6) (a) He looked at the picture.

     (b) He looked at it.

(7) (a) He *looked up* the word in the dictionary.

     (b) He *looked* the word *up* in the dictionary.

     (c) He *looked* it *up* in the dictionary.

例句 (6) 的 at 為介系詞,例句 (7) 的 up 為副詞。遇到介系詞時,即使受詞變成代名詞 it 也不會改變語句順序,如例句 (6) 的情形。例句 (7) 中,由兩個單字組成的 looked up 表現出一個及物動詞的功能,up 放在 the word 之前的 (a) 句,或者放在 the word 之後的 (b) 句都可以。但是,受詞的 the word 變成代名詞 it 時,就如 (c) 句中的 looked it up 一樣,必須放在兩個單字之間。再舉一個例子來看:

(8) (a) She had to *give up* all her friends.

      (b) She had to *give* all her friends *up*.

      (c) She had to *give* them *up*.

雙字動詞最大的功能之一,就是大多數皆可轉化成名詞,且多為可數名詞。將本單元開頭例句中的雙字動詞變成名詞性質後,即形成下列例句:

(1) Military *buildups* are reported in both countries./ Both countries are engaged in military *buildups*.

(2) His *pullout* from the agreement at the last minute angered all involved in the negotiations. （他在最後關頭退出協議，激怒了在場所有的與會人士。）

(3) The *breakoff* of diplomatic relations between the two countries will bring tension to the region.（兩國外交關係的斷絕將使該地區陷入緊張的情勢中。）

(4) The scandal came as a *letdown* to many of his supporters.

(5) The security force made a *crackdown* on the dissident groups.

雙字動詞和其名詞形之所以受人重視，是因為不管聽起來或看起來都讓人容易理解，且其含意範圍廣泛。接著再舉一個使用頻率相當高的雙字動詞及其名詞形 breakdown 為例（括弧內的詞語為比較正式的用字）：

(1) The massive power *breakdown* left hundreds of people trapped inside elevators. (= a sudden failure in operation)（大規模的停電使數百人受困在電梯裡。）

(2) Military observers reported a complete *breakdown* of morale among the soldiers. (= collapse, disintegration)（軍事觀察家報告說軍隊的士氣已經完全瓦解。）

(3) Repeated border clashes led to a *breakdown* of negotiations between the two countries. (= collapse,

failure)（國境不斷發生衝突導致兩國談判破裂。）

(4) He is suffering from a nervous *breakdown* after years of overwork. (= weakness, collapse)（經年累月的過度工作讓他精神崩潰。）

(5) Let me give you a *breakdown* of our budget request. (= analysis, classification)（讓我向您報告預算申請的明細。）

　　除了上述的意思之外，breakdown 還可以解釋為「化學的分解（作用）」(= chemical decomposition) 之意。

　　雙字動詞對以英語為母語的人來說，是在幼兒時期，也就是剛接觸語言時最先學會的東西，這成為他們日後語言行為的核心。通常大多數人開始學習英語這項外語是在國中以後，所以無法體驗到初學英語階段最重要的「幼兒時期」，可說是在不穩固的基礎上，一邊使用多音節的語彙及複雜的構句，一邊和英語糾纏不清。為了儘快鞏固英語的根基，我們應該更加重視雙字動詞，並視之為學習的寶貴之鑰。

　　由於雙字動詞的特徵為口語化，因此在如論文等注重形式的正式文章中要謹慎使用。不過，由於雙字動詞簡潔易懂，不僅常用在日常會話當中，甚至連在報紙、雜誌及廣播節目中都會頻頻出現。從 sit-in（靜坐抗議）, sing-in（聽眾參加的音樂會）, sleep-in（在公共場所的夜宿抗議）, break-in（非法入侵）, cover-up（掩護）, layoff（暫時解雇）, payoff（賄賂）, play-off（決定輸贏的比賽），到 blastoff, liftoff（皆指火箭發射）, countdown（倒數計時）, linkup（連結裝置）, splashdown（海上降落），甚至 meltdown（核能電廠反應爐爐心熔毀，引申指經濟崩潰）等，

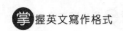

雙字動詞已在各種領域裡產生新的釋義，持續賦予英語新鮮感
與靈活性，可以說是英語活力的泉源。

9 各種強調的手法

當我們在會話或演講中想要強調自己想說的話時，通常會
放大音量、加重語氣、使用手勢或再三重複。在這些手法中，
只有重複的手法可以用於句子裡，當然也有其他強調的手法可
以運用到句子上。為了寫出簡潔有力、文采豐富且深具魅力的
文章，必須要將這些表現強調的方法銘記在心。在此列舉幾項
重要的強調手法。（強調的部分以斜體字表示）

（1） 重複單字。和會話及演講一樣，是最簡單的方法。

He talked *on and on and on*. （他喋喋不休。）

I just *keep pushing and pushing and pushing* to get what I'm
after.—[*Time*]（為了得到想要的東西，我會一而再再而三地追
求。）

The responsibility for the mistake is *mine, and mine only*. （這項
錯誤的責任只在我一個人身上。）

（2） 使用加強語氣的副詞、形容詞（片語）。

He is *way* ahead of the times. （他走在時代的尖端。）

I agree with you *100 percent*. （我百分之百同意你的看法。）

She is a *total* stranger. （她完全是個陌生人。）

He climbed the corporate ladder from the *very* bottom. （他從公

司的最基層慢慢爬升。)

（3） 使用 every, each, one and only 等字。

She was *every* inch Cherry Queen. （她是實至名歸的「櫻花皇后」。）

She prayed for his safe return *every single* day. （她每一天都在祈禱他平安歸來。）

I want to thank *each and every* member of our team for their hard work. （我要感謝這個團隊裡辛苦工作的每一位成員。）

This is the President's *one and only* view. （這是總統獨一無二的見解。）

（4） 使用 all。

The old man sat *all* by himself in a corner of the room. （老先生孤零零地坐在房間的角落。）

She was *all* smiles. （她笑容滿面。）

I'm *all* thumbs. （我真是個沒用的東西。）

He apologized in *all* sincerity. （他真心誠意地道歉。）

The cherry blossoms were in *all* their splendor. （櫻花開得繽紛絢麗。）

（5） 利用有加強語氣作用的名詞。如例句中帶有「化身」、「象徵」、「代表」 等意思的單字。 也可以用形容詞 incarnate, personified 接在名詞後面，不管這些名詞的內容是好的一面或壞的一面，皆可以使用。

She is *the embodiment* of elegance. (= She embodies

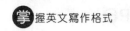

elegance.)（她是優雅的化身——無與倫比的優雅。）

He was *the incarnation* of greed.（他是貪婪的化身。）

He was evil *incarnate*.（他是惡魔的化身。）

He was courage *personified*.（他是勇氣的象徵。）

She was *the* [*very*] *picture* of happiness.（她是幸福的表徵。）

The boy is *the pink* of health. (= The boy is in the pink of health.)（這個男孩是健康的表徵。）

He is *the soul* of generosity.（沒有人比他更慷慨。）

注 1 ：除了 embodiment 之外，也可以使用 epitome, incarnation, model, personification。

注 2 ：She is elegance *itself*. 的意思和 She is the embodiment (*or* personification) of elegance. 一樣，也使用到強調的手法。

（6）　原本不必要的助動詞 do 和本動詞合併使用後，會產生強調的效果。

Do let me know when you get home.（回到家後，一定要聯絡我。）

I *did* call you, but there was no answer.（我真的有打電話給你，可是沒人接聽。）

（7）　將否定的代名詞或 no, not 放在句首。

Nothing will ever change his attitude toward us.（沒有任何事能改變他對我們的態度。）

No amount of pressure could obtain his confession.（無論施予多大壓力都無法使他招供。）

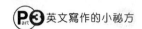

Not a soul was to be seen on the dimly-lit street. (昏暗不明的街道上看不見任何人影。)

（8） 同時使用 no 和加強語氣的 whatever, whatsoever。

I have *no intention whatever* of resigning until I have found a successor. (未找到接班人之前，我根本沒打算辭職。)

There is *no doubt whatsoever* about his sincerity. (他的真誠無庸置疑。)

The boy was beaten for *no reason whatsoever*. (這名男孩在毫無理由的情況下遭到毆打。)

（9） 利用否定形式的片語。

She said so *without a moment's hesitation*. (她毫不遲疑地說了出來。)

There was*n't a speck of* cloud in the sky. (天空萬里無雲。)

I would*n't give* the CD *for the world*. (說什麼我都不會交出這張 CD。)

She would*n't for the life of her* leave her children. (她絕對不會離開她的孩子。)

（10） 同時使用疑問詞和特殊的副詞片語。

What *in the world* is going on at this late hour? (時間都這麼晚了，到底發生什麼事？)

Who *on earth* told you about his affair? (到底是誰告訴你他外遇的事？)

What *ever* did you do to make her so angry? (你到底做了什麼

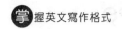

事讓她如此生氣？）

（11） 省略一部分比較級的句子。

He *couldn't be happier* [than he is now].（他高興極了。）

I *couldn't agree with you more* [than I can now].（我完全贊成你的意見。）

The timing of his visit to Japan *couldn't be worse* [than it is].（他訪問日本的時機實在很不湊巧。）

Americans *have never had it so good* [as they do now].（美國現在的景氣實在好得不得了。）

（12） 強調構句。基本形式是將強調的部分放在 It is...that (who, which) ～ 中有省略符號的地方。在這種構句之下，即使拿掉 It is 及 that 之後，也不會改變意思。以此種構句造句如下：

It is in winter *that* Mt. Fuji looks at its best.（富士山最美的時候是在冬季。）

It is only when we have our own children *that* we realize how much we owe our parents.（養兒方知父母恩。）

第二句即使改成以下例句，意思也不會改變。

(A) We do not realize how much we owe our parents until we have our own children.

(a) We only realize how much we owe our parents when we have our own children.

將 (A) 套進強調構句後變成：

(B) *It is* not until we have our own children *that* we realize how much we owe our parents.

最後再將此句中的 It is 和 that 抽離後變成：

Not until we have our own children we realize how much we owe our parents.

但因為這樣的構句不是一般常見的句子，所以主句中的 we realize 必須倒裝改成 do we realize。最後完成的句子如下：

(C) Not until we have our own children do we realize how much we owe our parents.

另一方面，也可將 (a) 句的主語和述語內副詞子句的順序顛倒，置換成下列句子：

(b) Only when we have our own children do we realize how much we owe our parents.

（13） 字序顛倒 (inversion of the word order)，即倒裝句。藉由變更一般的句子結構，以達到強調的目的。

如同在 (12) 項中的例句 (C) 和 (b) 所見，表示否定或強調的詞語通常置於句首。而且，主句的主語和述語的順序會顛倒。下列例句為二次世界大戰期間，英國首相邱吉爾 (Sir Winston Churchill) 致贈英國空軍們的一段讚美詞，讚揚他們英勇反擊當時處於優勢的德國空軍並成功奪回領空權的事蹟。

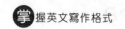

Never in the field of human conflict has so much been owed by so many to so few.（在人類的爭鬥中，從不曾有過這麼多的人因極少數人而受惠如此良多。）

這段讚美詞可說是倒裝句的標準範例。

Under no circumstances are public servants allowed to leak secrets obtained in the execution of their work.（不論在什麼情況之下，公務人員絕對不能將執行公務所得知的祕密洩漏出去。）

Seldom before in U.S. history has any President been so consistently rebutted by the legislators.—[*Time*]（美國歷史上幾乎未曾有過總統遭到全體議員一致反駁的情形發生。）

No sooner had the police pulled out than the demonstrators resumed throwing rocks.（警方一撤退，示威人士隨即又開始丟擲石頭。）

Little did I expect to see you today.（我萬萬沒想到今天會遇見你。）

（14） 運用最高級的強調手法。但即使是表最高級的單字，由於本身意義常被淡化，反而有時會造成強調性的不足。為了強調本身意義，可以使用其他的方法表達。茲列舉重要的方法如下：

(a) 以 by far 來強調和其他類似物的差別。另外亦可使用 far and away, by [all] odds, by a long shot。這些詞語都有「出類拔萃」、「遠遠超越一切」的意思。

Mt. Fuji is *by far* the most popular symbol of Japan. （富士山為最受歡迎的日本象徵。）

Football is *far and away* the most popular sport in much of South America. （足球運動特別受到眾多南美洲人民的熱烈喜愛。）

(b) 使用 ever, yet。

Beethoven is the greatest composer that the world has *ever* produced. （貝多芬是這個世界上最偉大的作曲家。）

He is the greatest composer that has *ever* lived.

He is the greatest composer *ever*.

At 77, John Glenn became the oldest astronaut *ever* to orbit the earth. （77 歲的約翰・葛倫成為環繞地球軌道最年長的太空人。）

It's going to be the biggest festival *yet*.（這項節慶即將成為有史以來最盛大的一次。）

(c) 加上 possible。

He asked me to finish the job in the shortest *possible* time.（他要求我儘量在最短的時間內完成。）

I look forward to your earliest *possible* response. （期待很快能得到您的回音。）

(d) 利用 single 突顯單一的特質。

Financial reform is the biggest *single* political issue in the current Diet session.（金融改革是當今國會最大的政治課題。）

Carbon dioxide is the *single* most important cause of air pollution. （二氧化碳是造成空氣污染的最主要原因。）

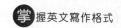

註：若同句中有 -est 的最高級出現時，表示強調的形容詞 single 要接在其後；若有以 the most 表示的最高級出現時，則放在 most 之前。

⑩ 避免重複的手法

不論是報章報導或電視新聞，都有重複使用某一個字詞的情形。不過，也許是習以為常了，大家似乎都沒有意識到。但在英文寫作上，最好還是避免重複用字。

「日本正經歷戰後最嚴重的經濟不景氣。不景氣的情況已經持續五年，仍不見有好轉的跡象。」

這段話中，「不景氣」被使用了兩次，若再長一點，很有可能會出現四次、五次。姑且不論內容如何，我們並不會特別去排斥這三個字；但若將此句譯成英文，變成下句：

"Japan is in the midst of the worst recession since the end of World War II. The recession has continued for five years, but no end is yet in sight."

即此段英文中使用了兩次 "recession"，如果再使用個四次、五次，相信一般都會感到厭煩。

是否可把第二次出現的 recession 改換成 it 呢？不過，由於句子的主詞為 Japan，所以 it 也可能指的是 Japan。直到看到了 for five years 時，才知道原來 it 指的是 recession。然而，讀者（或聽眾）在一瞬間 (for a split second) 會不容易分清楚 it 到底是指

哪一個英文字而感到混淆。

因此,第二次出現的 recession 最好不要換成 it。建議另以 the economic crisis 或 the business slump 來取代 ,或者以 the economic downturn, the sluggish economy 來代替。

在此並非意指當「不景氣」出現五次時,譯文中就也要更改五種替代詞。畢竟適合的替代字詞不是常常可以找得到,況且過度的置換只會產生不自然的反效果。不過,在重複使用同樣的字詞前,若能適當運用其他的字眼替代,將可以使文章更加富有變化。

此外,若「日本」也重複好幾次時,可將 Japan 換成 the nation (*or* country) ,而 Japan's 也可以改成 the nation's (*or* country's) ,也就是說能用最簡單又常用的說法來代替 ,例如定冠詞 the 就在此發揮了功效。

再舉出「美日關係」一例。這四個字翻譯成英文的基本說法為 Japan-U.S. relations。實際上還可以使用下列自基本型變化後的字詞替代 :

Japanese-American relations

relations between Japan and the U.S.

relations between Tokyo and Washington

relations between the world's two greatest economies

或者,也可以運用太平洋這個英文單字,將日本說成 on this side of the Pacific ,而將美國說成 on the other side of the ocean。

◆遣詞用字上的轉換

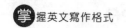

為了避免使用相同的措詞或重複性的說法，可從用詞和內容上來考量。

首先，所謂遣詞用字的轉換，就是指同義字 (synonym) 的活用。若是一開始能掌握好關鍵字，就算不是在一個同心圓裡的同義字也可以使用，只要在使用情境上的意思相同、類似即可。當然，當意思重疊性愈高時，就愈可以多多用來替代。

以「人員裁減」為例：

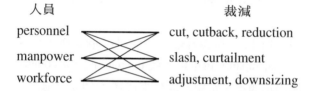

左邊和右邊不同單字的組合，可以產生數種表現方法。另外，當我們要具體地表示「解雇」的意思時，亦可用 discharge, dismissal, layoff（暫時解雇）等的名詞，或 dismiss, discharge, fire, sack, give the pink slip 等的動詞。

「選舉」可用 election, vote, poll，若還需要替代字，也可以使用 referendum。「車禍死者」則可用 traffic deaths, traffic fatalities, the death toll from traffic accidents 等字詞。

表示「國家」之意時，可使用 (1) 地理概念濃厚的 a country，(2) 帶有國民意識的 a nation，(3) 法律概念性強的 a state，(4) 重視軍事力量及經濟力量的 a power 等字詞表示。這些單字可以互相替代，但有時也會因意義明顯的不同而產生無法替代的情形。舉例如下說明這四種意義的不同：

(1) 和 (2) 可互相替代，例如 throughout the country (*or*

nation), the entire country (*or* nation)。但不能使用 (3)、(4)，若使用 (3)、(4) 來替代就會變得怪異。

在利用 (2) 造句的 The nation will go to the polls today to elect a new House of Representatives. （今天將舉行眾議院的選舉）句子中，不能改用 (1) the country 當主詞。這是因為要去投票所 (polls) 投票的人是「國民」的緣故。當然，也無法用 (3) 和 (4) 替代。

利用 (3) 造詞的 「愛好和平的國家」 在聯合國憲章 (U.N. Charter) 中稱之為 "peace-loving states"，這是由於國際法上國家均統一以 states 表示之故。而對於「主權國家」，除使用 sovereign states 之外，還可用 sovereign nations，有時也可用 sovereign countries 來取代。但是碰到「國家元首」the head of a state，「國家貴賓」a state guest 時，均不可用 (1)、(2)、(4) 代替。

(4)「軍事大國」、「經濟大國」一般各以 a [major] military power, a [major] economic power 表示，在包含「力量」的要義上，皆不適用 (1)、(2)、(3) 的說法。順便一提，「海軍國家」為 a sea power，而「超級強國」為 a superpower。

近年來甚至有愈來愈多如同此例 "A financial crisis hit the fast-growing economies in Southeast Asia." （金融危機襲擊經濟快速發展的東南亞各國） 的說法，是從經濟的觀點以 an economy 表示「國家」。

在尋找同義字時，務必要查閱 thesaurus （字彙分類辭典）或 English-English dictionary。

◆內容意義上的轉換

要將「美日關係」翻成英文時，可以 Tokyo 代表「日本」，

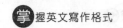

以 Washington 代表「美國」。這一點與其說是用字遣詞的**轉換**，不如說是內容意義上的**轉換**。

如果只是把「東京」翻成 Tokyo 就感到滿意，說實在地，這種譯法也未免太平淡無奇、缺乏寫作技巧了。因為東京既是 Japan's capital，又是 Japan's largest city with a population of close to 12 million，更是 the biggest financial market in Asia。所以從「美日關係」上來看，東京也可以用「日本」或「日本政府」替換。

另外，「京都」可以說是 the old Japanese capital，「橫濱」是 Japan's second largest city of 3.4 million，也是 a bustling port city with a soaring landmark tower on its waterfront，亦曾經是 the home to the Yokohama BayStars, the 1998 professional baseball champions。而北海道是 the northernmost island of the Japanese archipelago，富士山則是 at 3,776 meters Japan's highest and most famous mountain。

若只是寫給日本人看的英文，一提起地名「彥根」，就可以單純用 Hikone 表示，而「奈良時代」只要寫成 the Nara Period 也就夠了。但是，對於不了解日本國情的外國人來說，恐怕無法留下任何印象。如果在「彥根」後補充說明為 a city on the eastern shore of Lake Biwa in central Japan and known for its majestic castle，而「奈良時代」附加說明為 the eighth century 時，對閱讀者來說，才是個容易接受的訊息，也能帶來某些事物的聯想。

好比我們接到一封住在德國某城鎮裡的人所寄出的信。信上若有說明那個城鎮靠近 Bonn（波昂），在 Rhine（萊茵）河畔時，相信好奇心強的人也許會馬上拿出地圖比對，以確認該城

鎮的所在地。若再加上和 Beethoven（貝多芬）有某種關聯訊息的話，就更能引起閱讀者的興趣了。

我們在寫英文時，應該要能靈活地提供一些補充的資訊。當然，在撰寫自己國家的事物時，若手邊正有本地圖或歷史年表的話，將會有更大的助益。

內容意義上轉換的基本原則，就是要儘可能補充大量的資訊，並顧慮到增加文章變化的趣味性。此時，寫作者的想像力和細心程度都將受到考驗。若能在最後讓讀者覺得這是一篇用心書寫的好文章的話，必然會提升對作者的評價。

◆ "say" 的改寫

say 是最常被廣泛使用的單字之一，同時其可替代的說法也極為豐富。例如，在報導首相召開記者會的報紙及電視新聞中，應該用何種措詞才能貼切傳達「首相說～」這句話的意思呢？從「說」、「表示」、「說明」、「強調」、「斷言」到「主張」等，都是常用來表示「說」的字眼。我們母語可在有限的基本單字外，藉由添加副詞等方式來豐富用字的表達。例如寫成首相「得意地說」或「笑呵呵地說」。而英文即使不另外加上副詞等用字，也可以用一個單字傳達出比 say 更多元、更具體的意思。

The prime minister said, "I will lead the way in this endeavor, devoting my full strength to the task of remaking Japan into a country in which the people can believe and which offers them peace of mind."（首相表示：「為使日本再次成為一個人們可以互信且祥和的國家，本人將努力盡一切所能來率領完成這項使

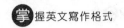

命。」） ——[引用 1998 年 8 月 7 日小淵首相的政治聲明演說]

上文若考量其為首相在國會所做的政治聲明 ，改用比 "said" 更有分量的 declared，或者有堅決之意的 pledged, vowed 及 emphasized 等字眼，皆為適當的選擇。而這些單字都可以接 that 子句引導的間接引述 (indirect narration)。也就是說成：

(1) The prime minister declared (*or* pledged) that he would lead the way in this endeavor....

而直接引述 (direct narration) 之後所能接的 "say" 的替代字，也有很多。

(2) "Who told you I did it?" he said. （他說：「誰告訴你那是我做的？」）

雖然這句話已表現出強烈的不滿，但另外，

(3) "Who told you I did it?" he demanded (*or* exploded).

很明顯地，demanded, exploded 都比 said 更有力量。

(4) "I didn't do it," he insisted (*or* protested).

insisted 則強烈地表達出否定他人對自身的懷疑之意，當然會比單純用 said 的效果好得多。

以下是取代 "say" 的單字，依其主要之意所做的大致分類。有 (*) 記號的動詞通常用在直接引述之後，很少用在直接引述之前。另外，下列動詞亦無法接間接引述；而沒有記號的動詞

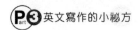

則可使用於直接引述之前或之後，也可以接間接引述。

例： cry(*)   "Help me!" she cried.

　　　　　　　（她叫喊著：「救命啊！」）

　　sigh(*)   "It's all over now," sighed our teacher.

　　　　　　　（「完了！」我們的老師嘆息著說。）

　　assert   He asserted, "I did what was right."

　　　　　　　（他堅稱：「我做的事是對的！」）

　　　　　　　"I did what was right," he asserted.

　　　　　　　He asserted that he had done what was right.

[比 say 較具堅定性、中立性的字] comment, note, observe, remark, state

[斷言] assert, declare, vow;（興奮）enthuse(*)

[主張] affirm, aver, charge, claim, contend, demand, insist, maintain;（爭論）argue

[強調] emphasize, stress

[說明，指出] explain, note, point out

[保證] pledge, promise, vow

[懇求] beg, plead

[抱怨] complain, grumble(*), moan

[抗議，反對] object(*), protest(*), remonstrate(*), retort(*)

[誇耀] boast, brag, bluster(*)

[激烈] explode(*), flash(*), fume(*), rage(*), rave(*), snap(*), snarl(*)

[興高采烈]　exult(*)

[微笑]　beam(*), chuckle(*), laugh(*), smile(*); smirk(*)

[嚎啕]　wail(*)

[同意]　agree, chime in(*), concur(*), consent

[回答]　answer, reply, respond

[附註，繼續]　add; continue(*), go on(*)

[坦白，承認]　admit, confess, confide(*); acknowledge, concede

[開玩笑，譏笑]　joke, banter(*), jest(*), sneer(*)

[叫喊]　call(*), holler(*)

[叫喊，吼叫]　cry, exclaim(*), howl(*), roar(*), shout, scream(*), shriek(*), squeak(*), yell(*)

[喘息]　gasp(*)

[嘆氣]　sigh(*)

[低聲說]　murmur(*), mutter(*); whisper(*)

[口吃]　mumble(*), stammer(*), stutter(*)

[單調的語氣]　intone(*)

Coffee Break

"Dash, 30, dash."

1998 年 10 月 1 日，白宮 Briefing Room（簡報室）的氣氛和往常截然不同。 這是因為四年來一直擔任柯林頓總統的 Press Secretary（新聞祕書，白宮發言人）

而聞名全美的 Mike McCurry（麥科里）在此舉行最後一次記者會。自 98 年初，總統與前白宮實習生的醜聞案浮出檯面以來，身為新聞祕書的他接連一段時日都成為記者們尖銳問題攻擊的眾矢之的。

儘管問題無關乎總統的內政、外交政策，僅只是些關於總統私生活的問題罷了。但對於必須回答這些險象環生的敏感話題的新聞秘書而言，這九個月來一定飽受煎熬。不過，還好美國身經百戰的記者們，都對於這一位總是竭盡所能誠實以對的新聞祕書給予高度的肯定。

最後一次的記者會中，仍舊是從總統的彈劾 (impeachment) 案通過決議之可能性的話題中展開。在近 50 分鐘的問答之後，有一位記者緩緩地說 "You leave with your honor intact."（你保留了完美的聲譽離開）。而 McCurry 則回答他 "Thank you. It's a good way to end."（謝謝你，這是一個好的結束）。

沒有比這兩句更感性的對話了。

"All right, enough. Dash, 30, dash."（好了，就到此結束。Dash, 30, dash.）McCurry 在說完這句話之後，隨即轉身離開 podium （講臺）。記者們一邊說 "Thank you." 一邊鼓掌歡送他。

將 Dash, 30, dash 寫成記號則為 —30—，表示「報導結束」 的意思。其起源已不明，不過據說是以前 telegraphers（電報員）發完電報後會標明的記號。以往我也曾經在打字原稿的結束處隨意加上這個記號。除了 Dash, 30, dash，還有 /// 和 # 都是用來表示「結束」

的意思。而 "Dash, 30, dash." 可以說正是 McCurry 對記者們親密道別的一句話。

參考書目及辭典

Associated Press, The *Stylebook and Libel Manual*, 6th Trade Edition, 1996.

Barnhart, Clarence L. and Robert K. Barnhart. *The World Dictionary*. Chicago: World Book, Inc., 1987.

Bastian, George C. *Editing the Day's News*. New York: Macmillan Co., 1956.

Cambridge International Dictionary of English. Cambridge University Press, 1995.

Collins Cobuild English Usage. HarperCollins Publishers Ltd., 1992.

Ehrlich, Eugune. *The Bantam Concise Handbook of English*. Bantam Books, 1986.

English, Earl and Clarence Hach. *Scholastic Journalism*, 7th Ed. Iowa State University Press, 1984.

Flesch, Rudolf. *How to Write, Speak and Think More Effectively*. The New American Library, 1963.

Quirk, Randolph, et al. *A Grammar of Contemporary English*. Essex: Longman, 1980.

Strunk, William Jr. and E. B. White. *The Elements of Style*. 3rd ed. New York: Macmillan Publishing Co., 1979.

Webster's Dictionary of English Usage, Springfield, Mass.: Merriam-Webster Inc., 1989.

《小学館ランダムハウス英和大辞典》（第 2 版），小学館，1994 年。
《新英和大辞典》（第 5 版），研究社，1980 年。

《新編　英和活用大辞典》，研究社，1995 年。

笹井常三《英文ライティング・ハンドブック》，研究社，1989 年。

ジエフリー・リーチ編著、田中春美、樋口時弘合譯《ネイティブ英語運用辞典》，Macmillan Language House，1996 年。

J. ジバルデイ、W. S.アクタート編著、原田敬一編譯《MLA 英語論文の手引》，（第 3 版），北星堂書店，1990 年。

引用資料出處

（[　]內為本書中省略出處名）

[Baker] Baker, Russell. *The Good Times*. Penguin Books, 1990.

[Bernstein] Bernstein, Carl. and Bob Woodward. *All the President's Men*. New York: Warner Paperback Library Edition, 1975.

[Capote] Capote, Truman. *The Grass Harp and a Tree of Night*. New York: Signet Book, 1951.

[Chang] Chang, Jung *Wild Swans: Three Daughters of China*. London: HarperCollins, 1993.

[Christie] Christie, Agatha. *Curtain*. New York: Pocket Books, 1976.

[Churchill-1] Churchill, Winston. *The Oxford Dictionary of Quotations*, 3rd Ed. Oxford: Oxford University Press, 1986.

[Churchill-2] Churchill, Winston. *The Penguin Book of Twentieth-Century Speeches*, edited by Brian MacArthur. London: Penguin Books, 1993.

[Emmott] Emmott, Bill. *The Sun Also Sets: The Limits to Japan's Economic Power*. New York: Random House, 1989.

[Galbraith] Galbraith, John Kenneth. *Economic Development.* Cambridge: Harvard University Press, 1967.

[Garrison] Garrison, Jim. *On the Trail of the Assassins.* London: Penguin Books, 1992.

[Hailey] Hailey, Arthur. *The Evening News.* London: Corgi Books, 1990.

[JFK] Kennedy, John F. *Let the Word Go Forth*, selected by Theodore C. Sorensen. New York: Delacorte Press, 1988.

[Keene] Keene, Donald. *Japanese Literature: An Introduction for Western Readers.* Tokyo: Charles E. Tuttle Co., 1977.

[King] King, Martin Luther. *The Penguin Book of Twentieth-Century Speeches*, edited by Brian MacArthur. London: Penguin Books, 1993.

[Kuralt] Kuralt, Charles. *Charles Kuralt's America.* New York: G. P. Putnam's Sons, 1995.

[Maugham] Maugham, W. Somerset. *Of Human Bondage.* New York: Modern Library, 1970.

[Mikes] Mikes, George. *The Land of the Rising Yen.* Penguin Books, 1975.

[Puzo] Puzo, Mario. *The Godfather. London*: Pan Books, 1969.

[Salinger] Salinger, J. D. *The Catcher in the Rye.* Penguin Books, 1958.

[Steinbeck] Steinbeck, John. *America and Americans*, New York: Viking Press, 1966.

[Thatcher] Thatcher, Margaret. *The Downing Street Years.* London: HarperCollins, 1993.

[VOA] Voice of America. *Words and Their Stories.* VOA Special

English, 1990.

[Vogel] Vogel, Ezra F. *Japan as Number One*. Cambridge: Harvard University Press, 1979.

[Waller] Waller, Robert James. *The Bridges of Madison County*. London: Mandarin Paperback, 1993.

[Ward] Ward, Kingsley G. *Letters of a Businessman to His Son*. Tokyo: Yohan Publications, Inc., 1989.

[WP-Press] The Washington Post. *Of the press, by the press, for the press, and others, too*. Boston: Houghton Mifflin, 1974.

報紙、雜誌

[*NYT*] *The New York Times*   [*AP*] *Associated Press*
[*WP*] *The Washington Post*   [*BBC*] *BBC on Air*
[*Times*] *The Times* (*of London*)   *Newsweek*
[*Independent*] *The Independent*   *Time*

一本簡單、好記，適合您隨時隨地翻閱學習的方便書

That's it!
就是這句話！

語言是要天天練才會順口，而且從愈簡單的句子著手愈有效。簡單、好記正是本書的一貫宗旨。我們知道您有旺盛的學習欲，但是有時候，心不要太大，把一句話練到熟就夠用了！

從身旁事物開始學習的
生活英語

每天食、衣、住、行所接觸到的事物，你知道如何用英文表達嗎？藉由學習身旁事物的英文用法，並在實際生活中不斷運用，使英文的生活用語能自然地留在腦海裡，不僅可以讓你輕鬆掌握日常生活的語彙，更可有效加強你的會話實戰能力，相信藉由本書，你會發現許多意想不到的樂趣。

21世紀英語學習貴在理解，而非死背！

英語大考驗

想知道你的文法基礎夠紮實嗎？你以為所有的文法概念，老師在課堂上都會講到嗎？由日本補教界名師撰寫的《英語大考驗》，提供你一個思考英語的新觀點，不管是你以為你已經懂的、你原本不懂的，還是你不知道你不懂的問題，在這本書裡都可以找到答案！

English test

打開話匣子
—Small Talk一下！

你能夠隨時用英語與人Small Talk、閒聊一番嗎？有些人在正式的商業英語溝通上應對自如，但是一碰到閒話家常就手足無措。本書針對此問題，教你從找話題到接話題的秘訣，讓你打開話匣子，輕鬆講英文。

社交英文書信

商務貿易關係若僅止於格式化的書信往返,彼此將永遠不會有深層的互動。若想進一步打好人際關係,除了訂單、出貨之外,噓寒問暖也是必須的。本書特別附有詳細的中譯及語句注釋,您千萬不可錯過!

活用美語修辭
——老美的說話藝術

日常生活中,我們經常引用各種譬喻,加入想像力的調味,使自己的用字遣詞更為豐富生動,而英語的世界又何嘗不是?且看作者如何以幽默的筆調,引用英文書報雜誌中的巧言妙句,帶您徜徉美國人的想像天地。

自然學習英語動詞
基礎篇

本書幫助您不需過度依賴文字解釋,就能清楚區分每個字彙特有的語感,切實掌握各個字彙不同的含義,進而使讀者能深切體會意象的道理,加以融會貫通,確實將英文字彙靈活運用在實際會話中。

English test

英語同義字辨析

一樣是「海峽」,channel 和strait 有何分別?

若以「規模」來說,答案是——channel > strait。有別於一般的同義字典,本書將具有同義性的字彙依「強度大小」、「程度高低」用「不等式(>)」的方式來表現,視覺化的標題設計,讓您一目瞭然!

國家圖書館出版品預行編目資料

掌握英文寫作格式 / 笹井常三著, 林秀如譯. — —初
版一刷. — —臺北市；三民, 民90
　　面；　　公分
參考書目：面
ISBN 957–14–3369–1　(平裝)

1.英國語言–作文

805.17　　　　　　　　　　　　　　　　90013758

網路書店位址　http://www.sanmin.com.tw

ⓒ　掌握英文寫作格式

著作人　笹井常三
譯　者　林秀如
發行人　劉振強
著作財
產權人　三民書局股份有限公司
　　　　臺北市復興北路三八六號
發行所　三民書局股份有限公司
　　　　地址／臺北市復興北路三八六號
　　　　電話／二五○○六六○○
　　　　郵撥／○○○九九九八——五號
印刷所　三民書局股份有限公司
門市部　復北店／臺北市復興北路三八六號
　　　　重南店／臺北市重慶南路一段六十一號
初版一刷　中華民國九十年九月
編　號　S 80334
基本定價　參元捌角
行政院新聞局登記證局版臺業字第○二○○號

ISBN　957–14–3369–1　(平裝)

林耀福等 主編 定價1500元

三民英漢大辭典

蒐羅字彙高達14萬字，片語數亦高達3萬6千。囊括各領域的新詞彙，為一部帶領您邁向廿一世紀的最佳工具書。

莊信正、楊榮華 主編 定價1000元

三民全球英漢辭典

全書詞條超過93,000項。釋義清晰明瞭，針對詞彙內涵作深入解析，是一本能有效提昇英語實力的好辭典。

三民廣解英漢辭典
謝國平 主編 定價1400元

收錄各種專門術語、時事用語達100,000字。例句豐富，並針對易錯文法、語法做深入淺出的解釋，是一部最符合英語學習者需求的辭典。

三民新英漢辭典
何萬順 主編 定價900元

收錄詞目增至67,500項。詳列原義、引申義，讓您確實掌握字義，加強活用能力。新增「搭配」欄，羅列慣用的詞語搭配用法，讓您輕鬆學習道地的英語。

三民新知英漢辭典
宋美璍、陳長房 主編
定價1000元

收錄中學、大專所需詞彙43,000字，總詞目多達60,000項。用來強調重要字彙多義性的「用法指引」，使讀者充份掌握主要用法及用例。是一本很生活、很實用的英漢辭典，讓您在生動、新穎的解說中快樂學習！

三民袖珍英漢辭典

謝國平、張寶燕 主編
定價280元

　　收錄詞條高達58,000字。從最新的專業術語、時事用詞到日常生活所需詞彙全數網羅。輕巧便利的口袋型設計，易於隨身攜帶。是一本專為需要經常查閱最新詞彙的您所設計的袖珍辭典。

三民簡明英漢辭典

宋美瑋、陳長房 主編
定價260元

　　收錄57,000字。口袋型設計，輕巧方便。常用字以＊特別標示，查閱更便捷。並附簡明英美地圖，是出國旅遊的良伴。

三民精解英漢辭典

何萬順 主編　定價500元

　　收錄詞條25,000字，以一般常用詞彙為主。以圖框針對句法結構、語法加以詳盡解說。全書雙色印刷，輔以豐富的漫畫式插圖，讓您在快樂的氣氛中學習。

謝國平 主編　定價350元

三民皇冠英漢辭典

　　明顯標示國中生必學的507個單字和最常犯的錯誤，說明詳盡，文字淺顯，是大學教授、中學老師一致肯定、推薦，最適合中學生和英語初學者使用的實用辭典！

莊信正、楊榮華 主編　定價580元

美國日常語辭典

　　自日常用品、飲食文化、文學、藝術、到常見俚語，本書廣泛收錄美國人生活各層面中經常使用的語彙，以求完整呈現美國真實面貌，讓您不只學好美語，更能進一步瞭解美國社會與文化。是一本能伴您暢遊美國的最佳工具書！

Sanmin English-Chinese Dictionary

三民英漢辭典系列

三民英語學習系列

U0022198